2021 Creative Writing Short Stories

A Collection of Short Stories
Written by Members
Of the Atria Willow Glen
Creative Writing Group

The design of this book was performed by Elvet E. Moore, an ATRIA resident, using the Creatspace Personal Computer Publishing System provided by Amazon.com.

Foreword

The Atria Willow Glen Creative Writing Group meets weekly with members writing short stories, which are shared with the other members at each meeting. To help stimulate the newer members to write a variety of short stories, the leader often passes out various clips known as writing prompts to be followed by them.

During the peak of the Covid-19 Virus Activity, the resident members did not always meet together as a group. However, the members did continue to write Creative Writing Stories, which they later shared with each other when the class was resumed.

Since its inception, the group has published seven different books containing numerous short stories. This eighth book contains stories that the members felt represented some of the best of their works. By collecting them together, they are able to share them with you.

Table of Contents

Table of Contents (pg 2)

Table of Contents (pg 3)

Virginia Braxton Stories

Keeping A Secret

By Virginia Braxton

Sharon heard someone say, "Can you keep a secret?" and was about to say, "Yes," when she realized the question was not addressed to her, but to one of the two women sitting on the patio just below her balcony.

Unlike many residents of the senior facility where she lived, Sharon had excellent hearing. She often overheard conversations not meant for her, but since most of them were complaints—food, weather, the time the mail was delivered, or the spinning of the earth on its axis, she had learned to ignore them. But this one sounded intriguing.

Voice No. 1 continued: "I'm so excited! Johnny and I are going to marry!"

Voice No. 2: "But who is Johnny?"

Voice No. 1: "My caregiver! He's so good to me and so, so, handsome!"

Voice No. 2: "Maudie! He's younger than your grandchildren!"

Maudie: "So what? He knows I can't give him children, and nobody pays attention to age differences any more, Carla."

Carla: "Well, what will your family say?"

Maudie: "We're going to elope and present them with a done deal. Friday morning we're going to take a taxi (Johnny doesn't have a driving license) down to the courthouse and get married."

Then Maudie and Carla moved out of Sharon's hearing and she sat thinking. She had seen Maudie and Johnny in the communal dining room, and wondered about them. Although Johnny wore caregiver garb, he did stand out from the other caregivers, and Sharon was not sure the reasons were good. True, he was very smooth, even handsome, but he seemed to radiate self-satisfaction at the same time he was being obsequious to Maudie.

Sharon had noticed previously that Maudie was forgetful, and Maudie's anecdotes about her life before she had moved to the facility indicated that she had plenty of money. Maybe that was the reason

Johnny was so attentive to her. Sharon knew that the caregivers in the section where Maudie and Sharon lived were privately hired by each individual (or family) and the management would not be able to intervene, even if it were so inclined. Sharon sighed. She could not think of a legitimate course of action to protect Maudie.

On Friday morning, Sharon was waiting at the desk to report that her bathroom faucet needed fixing when a man came in hurriedly and asked, "Does anyone know where my aunt Maudie is? I can't rouse her on her phone, and her caregiver doesn't answer either. I was supposed to meet with her this morning."

Sharon said, "Well, earlier this week I heard her say that she and Johnny were taking a taxi to the courthouse Friday morning to get married."

"Good heavens," the nephew said. "I've got to stop that farce!" As he rushed out, he called back, "What's your name? We'll talk later!"

"Sharon Dubinsky," Sharon called to his departing back. She did not see Maudie or Johnny for the rest of the day.

The next day she received a beautiful bouquet with a card, which said: "Thank you for saving the day. Please call me at this phone number. Signed, Tom Gibbons, Maudie's nephew."

Sharon called the number. Her first question was: "Is Maudie all right? I haven't seen her today."

Tom answered, "She's more or less all right. I arrived before the JP started the actual marriage. I said, 'Johnny, before you marry her, you should know that Maudie does not control her money. The bulk of it is in an unbreakable trust. The income from that trust is what she lives on, and I handle her finances, including dealing with the agency you work for. I am calling them NOW to tell them I am firing you! If you and Maudie want to continue with this marriage, I can't stop you, but I warn you, you both will be living on what you earn yourself.

'Well, Sharon, Johnny completely lost it, shouting, and cursing. I'm not sure that Maudie even knew what some of the words he used meant. He ended up screaming that SHE had led HIM down the garden path. He called her an ugly, pathetic old woman that he wanted nothing to do with, and stormed out.'

Aunt Maudie already was having hysterics, and at that she collapsed. We got her into the car and I took her for rest and evaluation to a facility that masquerades as a high end spa, but is really for borderline psychiatric patients."

"Will she be coming back here?" Sharon asked.

"I don't know for sure, but I doubt it," Tom replied.

"In any case," Sharon said, "There's no need for anyone else here to know the details of Maudie's elopement. I can keep a secret."

Pirates

By Virginia Braxton

Timmy burst into the house shouting, "Pirates! Pirates! Call the police!"

"For pirates you call the Coast Guard or the Navy, honey, not the police," said his mother.

"But they're real! I saw him. You have to call the police! He didn't have a big hat, but he took a package from the Anderson's porch!"

"Porch pirates!" exclaimed Tim's dad, looking up from his computer. "Tim, how could you see the Anderson's porch from here?"

"I was on lookout in my treehouse and I uh-borrowed your bird glasses and there's a hole in the leaves and I can see right through it to the Anderson's porch."

"OK. What happened?"

"The UPS truck came along and left a package at that grey house, and then one at the Anderson's. Then as soon as it turned the corner onto Green St., a black van came along. Someone got out, ran up, and took the package from the grey house, and then the one from the Anderson's! He didn't have a real pirate hat, just a hoodie."

"Well," said Tim's dad, "You're right. We should call the police, even if it turns out that there's not

17

much they can do." He picked up his phone. "Yes, this is Arthur Malcolm, 1555 Central Ave. and my son just witnessed a porch piracy at the Anderson's house on Oak Street. They're friends of ours. Most of the family is away visiting grandparents, and Don works downtown, so it's empty in the daytime. My son saw it from his tree house. The thieves got away in a black van." Turning to Tim he asked, "Is there anything more you can tell us about the van? Maybe the model?"

"No," Tim sighed, "and I couldn't even write down the whole license number. See?"

"He got a partial license plate number," said Tim's dad, and repeated it to the dispatcher. "Yeah, I think he's pretty smart." He listened for a bit, and then said, "OK. We'll look for you later in the afternoon."

"Tim," said his dad, "the police think you did a good piece of work and want to talk to you about it. They'll come over later in the afternoon, but they've some other things to do first."

Later that afternoon Officer Gonzalez, who arrived in a patrol car, introduced himself to Tim and his family. He asked to see the license plate numbers Tim had recorded and Tim showed him how he had written them on the treasure map he was drawing, which was the only paper and pencil he had in the treehouse. Officer Gonzalez said that a black van with a license plate starting with the numbers Tim had recorded was reported stolen that morning and had not yet been recovered. He asked to see where Tim had been when he recorded the numbers. When Tim took him to the tree house, Gonzalez looked inquiringly at Tim's dad, who said, "It's safe for adults." Then turning to Tim, Gonzalez saluted and said, "Permission to board, sir?"

Tim returned the salute, and said, "Permission granted," and together they climbed into the tree house. Then Tim showed him where to find the opening in the leaves and Officer Gonzalez used the birding glasses to look at the Anderson's front porch, and made a few notes.

After they left the treehouse, Officer Gonzalez promised to get back to them and left.

Back at the police station, Officer Gonzalez reported to the Chief. "There's no doubt about it, you can see the porch from the kid's tree house. There's an opening in the leaves at just the right point. Perfect place for a stakeout."

"We're in a bind," the chief said. "There are a lot of packages being stolen in that neighborhood, and UPS is getting testy about it. I'd like to stop it, but I just don't have the manpower to put into it, even if I could figure how to do it."

"It's a pity to waste such a good place for a stakeout," mused Gonzalez, whose childhood had not included treehouses. Then his face brightened. "What about the Police Cadets? They're young enough to look natural up in a tree house, and they're large enough to handle that camera, which is almost as big as Timmy. I'll bet they'd be thrilled to give us a hand in real police work. We could make them junior deputies or something."

"It's an idea," said the Chief. "Let me think about it."

A few days later Timmy saw another pirate raid. This one was not on the Anderson's porch, but on the grey house. Again, Timmy was only able to get a few license plate numbers and the car had been stolen earlier that day. That evening Tim's dad was telling Don Anderson about the excitement, and Don was surprised to hear that packages were being delivered to that house. He had thought the house was empty but that a landscaping agency was having the grass cut and the property groomed. He had never seen anyone coming or going from the house. They dutifully passed along that information to Officer Gonzalez.

Don thought it would be fun to mix things up a little bit, and started ordering things, which would be delivered by UPS.

Then the police chief called to say that the next day Officer Gonzalez would be bringing over two police cadets who, with Timmy's (and his parent's) permission, would be using the tree house as their observation post.

Timmy was disappointed that the cadets, Sam and Louie, were not in uniform, but they said that their plain clothes were part of their cover. Timmy thought that their camera looked as big as a cannon, but they hoisted it up and pointed it through the opening in the leaves. They explained that the camera was digital, recorded instantly with a powerful zoom lens, so the pictures taken with it would really help get information about the thieves.

Timmy was delighted to have their company. They made sure that one of them was always watching, and soon realized that there was a pattern. If UPS only delivered a package to the Anderson's, the porch pirate did not come. If the grey house got a package, the UPS truck was hardly out of sight before the pirate had taken it. If the Andersons had a package that day, he took that too. Further, the packages for the grey house were always the same relatively small size and ten days apart. The chief grew very thoughtful when he heard that.

One day the chief sent a message to Timmy, his parents, and the cadets, asking them to meet him at the station that evening. They were shown to a meeting room where there were not only the Chief and Officer Gonzalez, but also some people in uniforms and others in street clothes who were identified as customs officers. The head customs officer said that tomorrow was the tenth day and they were planning to capture the porch pirate. They had evidence that what was happening in their town was just the tip of the iceberg and wanted to interrogate him. Therefore, very, very, early in the morning, Timmy and his family might see some strange people in the neighborhood, but not to worry. And whatever else happened, tomorrow they were absolutely to stay indoors and out of the tree house. He asked them to promise to do that, and they did.

Timmy barely fell asleep before breakfast time, and then Sam and Louie arrived, but they had to come inside. They all complained that they would have a better view if they were in the tree house, but it was full of customs officers, so they played board games in the living room. Finally, they heard shouts, cars roaring and police sirens, but Timmy's dad held them to their promise to stay inside.

At last Officer Gonzalez came to the door. He said that they had captured the porch pirate who was a young man from the other side of town, and at the same time, they had made a raid in the next county. The customs officer came over and thanked them. He said the smugglers were bringing in pills which they sold cheaply compared to what the legal ones sold for in this country. He said the smuggled ones were badly made and had contaminates in them, but people didn't care and bought them anyway. He said Timmy and the cadets had been a great help and thanked them for their service.

As he turned to leave, Tim's dad said quietly to him, "What kind of pills were they?"

"Ersatz Viagra," he responded.

Buttons

By Virginia Braxton

Harry watched as Sally plunked a five-gallon can on the table. He contemplated the can rather than pulling the lid off.

Speaking in the tone of voice that only fifty years as Harry's older sister could explain, she said, "Come on! Don't be such a dawdler, Harry!"

They were cleaning out their mother's house, and she really wished it had not fallen to Harry to "help" her, but he had the most flexible schedule of their siblings. He was on break from the experimental education program where he taught, and everyone else had to work. But, he had to touch, feel, and reminisce about every article that Sally or he found. He wanted to keep everything. Now he was living near Sally in a small house, which was rapidly filling up.

Harry shook the can. It rattled. "The can is really heavy. What do you suppose is in it? Spanish doubloons?"

"Well take the lid off and find out," she snapped. Buttons!

Every kind of button, all jumbled together. All sizes and colors, some on cards, some loose, and some in white envelopes with labels such as "1940 Mama's blue dress."

"Well," said Harry, "Mom always said never throw out a button, but it looks as though Grandma and Great Grandmother said the same thing, and all that they saved are right here. Some might be collector items."

"But those beige plastic ones are still on the cards. They can't be worth anything."

"Maybe they are left over from when Uncle Tom was a tailor. I'll sort them."

"Not now!" said Sally, throwing the loose buttons back in the can and slamming the lid on. "We've work to do."

"I'll take them home," said Harry, and he took the can out to his car. Sally shook her head. No wonder Harry's wife had left him.

Later that evening, Harry put the big can in the middle of his dining room table and began pulling out buttons. He was delighted to find two which matched the eyes on the stuffed dog his Mother had made him. They were special. The next was a card of black buttons, obviously from Uncle Tom. Then there were two matching black and rose cloisonné buttons on shanks. And some that looked to be genuine tortoise shell.

He started sorting by putting all the ones still on cards together. Then he thought he could sort by color. However, a big button was different from a small button, even if the small one was the same design. In addition, some on cards were similar to ones not on cards. Soon the table was covered with buttons, but there were very few piles. He sat looking at them. There was a suggestion of a pattern. He moved a few to make the pattern clearer. Then he moved some more. But some were metal and had shanks, so they could not lie flat. Well, he could get rid of the shanks. He got out his metal shears and went to work. However, cutting off the shanks wasn't easy, and if he did that, how would he fasten the buttons to the background? Best hold off eliminating the shanks. He had in mind swirling rich colors for the background, with the buttons as highlights or points of interest.

For the next few days, Harry spent every spare moment playing with buttons, eating standing up so he would not disturb the patterns emerging on the table. The buttons reminded him of chips of mosaic, but lighter. He stretched a canvas and painted what he saw as the background—pomegranate, orange, and blue swirls.

While he waited for the paint to dry, he explored buttons on the internet. He learned that there were people who collected rare buttons and had conventions where they exhibited and sold or exchanged their buttons. He also learned that there were people who covered their clothes solidly with buttons for decoration. He wondered how they sat down.

Once the paint was dry, he began arranging the buttons on the background, but since he was not sure what he was doing, he waited to glue them. Then he stumbled against the background panel and many of the buttons shifted, but he liked the new pattern better, so he glued them that way.

When school was back in session, Harry was still obsessed with buttons. One day one of his students asked him what he did when he wasn't in school.

"First, I correct homework, and then I play with buttons," he answered.

"Buttons?"

"Yes, buttons." Harry launched into an enthusiastic sharing of all he had learned about buttons, becoming so enthralled that he used up half the math period.

"My mom has a lot of buttons. I'll ask her for some for you," volunteered a student.

Buttons took on a life of their own in Harry's classroom. He had to make a strict rule, which the students helped him enforce, that all the schoolwork had to be completed before the word "button" was mentioned. He noticed, to his delight, that not only did his students complete their schoolwork more quickly but also it was improving. They were more attentive and seemed to understand it better.

But there wasn't enough time. With the principal's help, he negotiated to have his students leave on the last bus, which gave them an extra half hour to work.

Many of Harry's students brought buttons from home to add to the piles. He noticed signs of a conspiracy among the boys who had not brought buttons, and he thought he'd better keep an eye on them.

Then one Monday morning the conspirators marched in glowing with triumph and dragging heavy bags. They cleared off a table and spilled out their bags on it, revealing piles of pottery shards in all colors as well as remnants of colored glass, possibly from old Coke bottles.

"We didn't have buttons," Kevin said, "but we found these in a dump near that abandoned factory on Third Street. Maybe we could use these instead of buttons."

"Great!" said Harry, barely containing his excitement. "Making patterns and pictures with small pieces of stone or pottery is an ancient art called mosaics. I'll have to get some books about mosaics, not for you to copy, but so you learn about the history of your art."

"We could make pictures on the walls," said Kevin, "then this room would be more cheerful."

Harry thought a moment about what the school district might say. "I think I can get some wooden panels we could use, and then display the panels here. That way we could decorate the walls, but if we needed to, we could clear the walls without having to chip off the stones, buttons, and pieces of glass."

On Saturday, Harry was carrying the first two blank panels he had made into the classroom when he ran into the principal.

"Harry!" said the principal, I'm glad you're here. I just received the official results for your class on the reading and math tests! Your students' scores are moving up the percentiles! Congratulations. I don't know what you're doing, but keep on doing it. What are those for?" pointing to the panels.

Harry explained about buttons and his students wanting to decorate the walls of their room, and the principal agreed with Harry that panels were the solution, and that they should go ahead with the project.

In the meantime, some of the students were curious about the history of the abandoned pottery factory and began to research it, planning to write a report when they had gathered as many facts as possible.

One day the principal asked Harry to stop by and see him after school.

"What's up?" asked Harry, as he entered the principal's office.

"It's complicated," said the principal. "You know, because we are running a special program, the legislative committee which authorizes the money evaluates the outcomes of a sampling of schools at end of the year. This year we are one of those schools."

"But you said we were doing well," interrupted Harry.

"We are, but there is a division in the committee. One faction wants to write glowing reports and expand the program. The other faction feels that there is a lot of money being wasted and wants to kill the program. The media has noticed the controversy and a television crew is following the committee around. As you know, I want them to see your room and meet your students. But since the TV crews will be there, we have to get written permission from a parent of each and every one of your students for them to be on television. Think you can do that?"

Harry explained the situation to his class and added that anyone who did not turn in a permission slip would have to spend the time in the library out of sight of the TV crew when it came. He had a remarkable 100% return rate, although privately, he had doubts about some of the signatures.

On the day of the visitation, the TV crew came before the students arrived and photographed the panels, which were on the walls. Later, when the students had settled, the visitors entered the room. The principal introduced Harry and his students to the evaluating committee and the TV crew (which was trying to be as inconspicuous as possible).

The student committee which had researched the defunct pottery factory, gave its report. The mosaic makers explained the history of mosaics and how they had to use math to figure the angles to cut the mosaics. Kevin stood up and said, "Look how beautiful our room is now!" The committee applauded.

That evening the local TV station had a segment on the "jewel of a school," and gave a recording of the program to the school. Later, the panels were exhibited at a very local art fair. Also Harry found that there was a market for his smaller "button scapes."

Green Menace

By Virginia Braxton

Herman threw his arms up defensively as the green tentacle-like arms tried to wrap themselves around him. He had seen these giant mutant ferns in the other parts of the maze he was stumbling around in, but this was the first time he had been attacked by one. Its fuzzy spikes looked soft, but were sharp, and now his hands and arms were bleeding. He kicked as hard as he could at its lower part and stepped back quickly, stumbled, and fell. As he struggled off the ground, he saw the fern had not moved any closer to him, which might mean that somewhere at its base, it was vulnerable.

He looked around and spotted a small stone gnome, which was holding a spear. He picked it up. It was heavy and unwieldy, but it extended his reach about two feet. Holding it, he approached the fern cautiously. As he bent to stab its bottom, its tentacles wrapped themselves around his neck, choking and scratching him. He used both hands to push the gnome's spear as hard as he could into the fern's base. The tentacles around his neck loosened and he wrenched himself free. He took a few steps away and saw with relief that the fern was collapsing like a punctured balloon.

He wanted to get away, even if it was only to another dead end, but as he turned toward the entrance, he saw the green walls closing off that escape route. Still holding the useful gnome, he threw himself into the diminishing gap and pulled both of them out on the other side.

"Thank you," said the gnome. "I was tired of that cul-de-sac, but I can't move on my own."

"What difference does it make?" asked Herman. "All of the cul-de-sacs are just alike."

"Oh, no," said the gnome. "There are very subtle differences, and some of them can guide us. You don't object to carrying me, do you?"

"Of course not," said Herman. "Not if it will get us out of here. I've been wandering in this maze as long as I can remember. By the way, I'm Herman. What should I call you?"

"Just call me Guide," said the gnome.

The clue as to which way to turn was embedded in the greenery opposite to the entrance of each space. Herman had to carry the gnome, whose eyesight was not very good, almost to that wall, and then lift him up to about where Herman's eyes were. If he found a tiny coral berry mixed in the greenery, it meant that Herman should turn left when he exited that space. If he found a vine with small white flowers, they should turn right on leaving. If both were there, they should go straight. Now that he knew what to look for,

Herman could find the clues, but Guide always insisted on being lifted up so he could verify Herman's decision. At last, they emerged from the maze.

"Thank you, Guide," said Herman. "I am going to go home now. Do you want to go back into the maze, or find another garden—my sister has a fairly nice one, or what?"

"I'm tired of gardens," said Guide. "Can I live with you?"

"But I live in a high-rise," said Herman. "I don't even have a balcony."

"Fine," said Guide. "I've had enough greenery. I'll be happy in the living room." So Guide became Herman's permanent roommate, but Herman's friends called him "Guido."

Dead

By Virginia Braxton

"Lynnie! Lusting after some glitz?"

Marylyn turned to see who was speaking to her and fainted, cracking her head on the pavement.

The next thing she knew she was being wheeled into the ER at the hospital.

"Are you on blood thinners? Did you feel dizzy? Are you diabetic?" the EMT asked.

"I saw a dead man I used to know. I want to call my husband! Where's my purse?" Marylyn responded.

****

Leon sat in a greasy spoon several blocks from Chicago's Michigan Avenue, drinking coffee and mentally kicking himself. He had been so startled to see Lynnie that he forgot himself and spoke to her. Now, he idly Googled her. To his surprise he found that she owned and operated a firm that specialized in recycling grease and oils. Who would have thought?

Well, he had an appointment to go to. He had not wanted to risk the heavy security in the Jewelers Row building where the diamond merchants worked, so they were meeting at the nearby McDonalds.

****

Marylyn was settled in bed in a hospital gown, when Tom rushed in.

"Honey, what happened? Are you all right?"

"They're afraid I have a concussion, so they want to keep me here overnight for some tests. My head does hurt. I hit it when I fainted."

"But what happened?"

"Oh, Tom, I was on Michigan Avenue, looking in the Cartier's window and laughing at the incongruity of diamonds with my recycling business, when a man said, 'Lynnie, lusting after some glitz?' When I looked at him it was Leon! He's the only one who ever has called me Lynnie, and it sounded and looked just like him! But he's dead! He disappeared ten years ago!"

Marylyn started to cry.

"Honey, let me get this straight. You were window shopping on Michigan Avenue and someone whom you believe to be your dead husband spoke to you."

"Yes."

"We'll get to the bottom of this, but, oh, how I wish I had met you before he did," Tom said.

"Sweetheart, I wouldn't have appreciated you then. And now I don't want to give you up for anyone else. I think I'm frightened."

Tom reached over and hugged her. "Look, I'm a lawyer, remember? I made damn sure before we married that all the legalities were taken care of. I never quite understood why you hadn't divorced

Leon for desertion, but since you hadn't and enough time had passed, he was declared legally dead. No bigamy. You may be his widow, but you're my wife now."

"I wonder if he wants the money I inherited from his mother. There's quite a bit of it."

"True," said Tom, "but we've always kept it entirely separate from our own finances. We never spent a cent of it. I don't know what the law would be in these circumstances, but if you had to give up the money, we could, without hardship.

"Now, is there anything you want me to bring you? I'm going to swing by the apartment and pick up stuff so I can spend the night here with you." And, he thought, I'll make a few phone calls while I'm at it.

At the apartment, he packed up a few things and then called the Police Department number he had for Sargent Chandler. Chandler had handled the missing person investigation on Leon and had followed the case all the way through to what they had believed was the end. Tom thought he would be interested in Marylyn's encounter.

Chandler most definitely was. "It never felt right to me, which is why I kept the files, even after Leon was declared dead. How is Marylyn taking this?"

"She's very upset, is certain it was Leon, and admits to being frightened."

"Where did you say she was when he spoke to her?"

"Michigan Avenue in front of Cartier's."

"Excellent! The Department works very closely with all those high-end jewelers. Give me your cell number and I'll get back to you."

Tom was at the hospital watching a hockey game with Marylyn when Chandler called.

"Security detail at the store remembered the event very clearly—any commotion in front of the store makes them nervous. They were the ones that called 911.

"They have three cameras and they gave me copies of the surveillance tapes from an hour before to an hour after the incident. When do you think Marylyn would be able to watch them?"

Tom wanted to put it off until the next day, but Marylyn was anxious to see what Chandler had. He arrived carrying a laptop.

"Hello, Marylyn," he said. "Are you sure you feel up to this?"

"I'd feel worse if I didn't watch it. Let's start."

Chandler picked the tape looking from the inside out the store window, and fast-forwarded to the point where Marylyn's face appeared. A man appeared behind her and spoke.

"That's him!" said Marylyn. "It's that same self-satisfied smirk I used to think was cute."

"The bastard!" exploded Tom. "He didn't even try to catch you or break your fall! Just turned and ran!"

"But why? Why is he doing this?" cried Marylyn.

"Marylyn," soothed Chandler, "We don't know what's going on, but we'll try to find out.

"I'll take the tapes—there are nine hours of them to see if there are any other clues or if he was hanging around the store."

Just then, a doctor came in to ask Marylyn how many fingers he had and where they were, so Chandler left, promising to stay in touch.

It was late afternoon the next day when Chandler called Marylyn at home asking if he could come see her.

"Of course," replied Marylyn, and Tom just walked in the door. Chandler arrived looking rather grim and tired. "Marylyn, have you heard anything from Leon?" he asked.

"Of course not. I would have called you if I had. Has something happened?"

"Well, we found a body and there's a chance it may be Leon's."

"And you want me to identify it?"

"No. This body can't be identified visually. By any chance, do you still have anything which would have Leon's DNA? We have his old dental records, but they're probably outdated now, and anyway DNA would be more certain."

"I might. Tom, can you please get me that box of stuff left over from when I cleaned out Leon's mother's place?" Marylyn asked.

Tom brought the box and Marylyn rummaged in it until she found a small, yellowed envelope. As she handed it to Chandler, she said, "I kept it because I just couldn't throw it out. I didn't know what to do with it." It was labelled "Leon's baby hair," and held two very soft brown curls.

"Bingo!" said Chandler putting it in an evidence bag.

"Marylyn," he continued, "we would like to put an undercover person at your plant. Can that be done without being too conspicuous?"

"Wait a minute," Tom broke in, "Is Marylyn in danger, or are you using her as bait?"

Chandler sighed. "We are not using her as bait. We're trying to protect her. We don't know if she's in danger, but near the unidentified body, we found a phone someone had used to Google her. I have the feeling that Leon was on the periphery of a much larger operation that we don't know much about yet."

"I could use some help right now," said Marylyn. "Jorge had to go to a funeral in Mexico, so I'm understaffed. Does your agent do unpleasant dirty work?"

"He will, if it's part of his cover," affirmed Chandler. "Does that mean you agree?"

Tom and Marylyn exchanged glances and nodded in agreement.

"OK," said Chandler. "I think you should meet off-site. I'll call him now."

A while later Marylyn answered the phone and the doorman said, "You have a UPS delivery here. Shall I send him up?"

"UPS?" repeated Marylyn and saw Chandler make a thumbs up sign. "Yes, send him up. Thank you."

A few moments later when the apartment doorbell rang, Chandler answered it and admitted a burly man in a UPS uniform carrying a large package. Turning to Marylyn and Tom, Chandler said, "I want you two to meet Sergio Zurowski, who will be protecting Marylyn.

"Sergio, I want to introduce you to Tom and Marylyn Clarke. Marylyn is the former wife and widow of Leon Bergamo who seems to have miraculously, but briefly, resurrected himself."

Tom asked Sergio, "Are you, or will you be armed?"

"Yes," said Sergio. "As a federal law enforcement agent I am armed now and will be when I am on duty. Will that be a problem?"

Tom noted with interest that the matter was no longer confined to CPD jurisdiction.

"I don't think so," responded Marylyn. "Most of the work is outside and now that the weather is cold, everyone's pretty well bundled up."

After they had rehearsed the cover story for Sergio, they agreed that Marylyn would go in early to meet her "new employee" and introduce him to the other staff members.

The next few days went smoothly at the plant until Kevin, another staff member, came into Marylyn's office, and asked to talk to her.

"Of course," agreed Marylyn. She had considerable respect for Kevin, a lanky redhead, who was taking a gap year working for her before, graduate studies in environmental economics.

"Marylyn, that new guy, Sergio, he's packing."

Marylyn blinked at Kevin, "Packing?"

"You know, carrying a gun."

"Oh," Marylyn paused. "Kevin, I know for a fact, that it's legal."

"You trust him?"

"Yes, he's well vouched for. I'm not free to share with you any details of what's going on, but if he gives you an order, obey it. Fast!"

"OK, boss lady," said an obviously curious Kevin as he went outside and back to work.

That same evening, Chandler dropped by to see Tom and Marylyn, looking grimmer than ever, and exhausted.

"Marylyn, I'm sorry to tell you that the DNA evidence shows that the body was Leon's."

Tom reached for Marylyn's hand, and Marylyn nodded.

"As far as we can determine, you are the only person with even the slightest claim to his body. Would you permit us to keep the identification a secret for a few more days?"

"It's all right with me. Will we be able to have a proper burial later?" inquired Marylyn.

"Certainly."

Two days later Sergio came into Marylyn's office and announced, "I'm sorry to give you such short notice, but today's my last day."

"Does that mean it's all over?" queried Marylyn.

"Yeah. It'll be on the news tonight. Say, that Kevin kid is sharp. I thought he'd made me, but then he turned helpful. Did you talk with him?"

"I had to," replied Marylyn.

Tom made a point of being home in time to watch the evening news with Marylyn. They were comfortably seated with a drink in hand when it came on.

"Local and federal law enforcement officials held a joint news conference today announcing that they had broken up a ring smuggling illegal blood diamonds into the United States. In connection with that, they made arrests for the murders of Antoine Carpentier, who had an office in the famed Jewelers Row, and his accomplice, Leon Bergamo. Carpentier's body was found in his Homewood house where his "safe room" had been broken into and the safe emptied. The thieves, however, had not found a cache of diamonds hidden in the leg of a pool table."

"Well," said Tom, "I'm glad that's over. How do you feel?"

"Relieved. I think I'll have what's left of Leon cremated, and bury the remains next to his mother, with a plaque that just gives his name and real dates."

Mistaken Identity?

By Virginia Braxton

Tom Constantini sat at his desk in the local FBI office, wishing that malefactors wouldn't produce such a volume of paperwork. As he reached for the first file, his phone rang.

"This is Inspector Gallagher of Metropolitan Homicide. We've had a shooting and your agent, Andrew Fuller, was just a few yards away and first on the scene. Will you liaise?"

"On my way!" Tom responded. As he drove to the site of the killing, he speculated. Andy was a forensic accountant, currently working on the deliberately tangled affairs of an import-export company. The documents he had been using were things like corporate tax returns, import declarations, and shippers export declarations, which had been available without a warrant. Could he have stumbled onto something to provoke a violent response?

At the site, he identified himself to the homicide detective who brought him to Andy who was sitting in a squad car drinking a cup of coffee. "Andy, I'm glad you are OK. Can you tell me what happened?"

"I was in my zone, running, when I came round the corner over there, and stumbled, literally, on him.

He was still bleeding, so I did what I could and called 911, but he died anyway."

"When you were running, did you hear a shot?"

"Tom, it's firecracker season. If I heard it, I dismissed it as another one of those damned illegal fireworks."

"Assuming the papers on him are actually his, he was Charles Brewer, and he lived in a building next door to the one I live in."

"OK. Did Brewer say anything?"

"Nope, he just gurgled and died."

Tom stood looking from Andy to Brewer and back again. Each was a youngish man, white, fit, medium height, short light brown hair, wearing khaki running shorts, and a "Save the Whales" tee shirt. Except for the fact that Brewer was dead and Andy was alive, they looked remarkably similar. Was Brewer shot by mistake for Andy? Tom sighed.

"Andy, we're going to have to keep you out of sight until we can sort this out. Give me the keys to your apartment so someone can collect your things. I'll drop you at the office so you can use your office e-mail to tell your family and friends that you are on an assignment and to communicate with you there. Then we'll stow you safely away."

The next day, Andy was doing push-ups to relieve his sense of confinement, when Tom stopped by.

"Well, Tom, what have you found out about Brewer?" he queried.

"So far, nothing special. He was a middle school science teacher, single, and so well liked that the principal is bringing in grief counselors for his students. He lived well within his means, in fact, was saving money. They said he didn't teach last summer and wasn't planning to this summer, so maybe that's why he was saving money.

"For public consumption, the police are handling the investigation, and the Bureau is not involved. In fact, we're actually communicating closely and freely. Obviously, our first priority is to find out whether you or Brewer were the intended target. His parents are driving up from downstate and we'll be meeting with them tomorrow. Maybe they'll know something that will help."

The next day, the police detective interviewed Brewer's parents with Tom and Andy (whom he simply introduced as "my colleagues Tom Constantini and Andy Carpenter") as quiet observers. The detective started, "Mr. and Mrs. Brewer, I want to offer our condolences on your loss. I want to assure you, that we're doing everything we can think of to bring your son's killer to justice. Frankly, I'm mad as hell, and want justice for your son.

"Did Charles have any enemies that you know of? Was there anyone who might wish to harm him?"

"No," said his mother wiping her eyes, "Not unless it's connected with his summer work."

"Tell us more about that."

"Well, for the last two summers, (and he would have gone this summer if he had lived), Chuck had gone to the Mississippi Delta and worked with a voter registration project. We knew it was dangerous. He said that there were threats against the organization, but he felt strongly about doing it. Being white, he worked almost entirely behind the scenes and tried to go off the grid to draw as little attention to himself as he could, but still, anyone doing that kind of work is in danger."

"Thank you, ma'am" said Tom, "That opens up a whole new avenue for us to explore."

As she was leaving, Mrs. Brewer turned to Andy and said, "You know, you look a lot like my son."

Later that day Tom contacted the Bureau's Jackson office to find out what they knew about Charles Brewer's organization, "Votes Make Right" (VMR).

He was told: "Well, one of their field workers, George Gregory, was assassinated yesterday. They'd had no warning. He was just shot dead on the street."

"And another one here, also without warning," sighed Tom. "What about Alabama?"

"Them, too. A field worker for VMR. This looks nasty, being in at least three different states and coordinated. Washington's assembling a special team and I'll instruct them to include your office."

When Tom stopped to see Andy the next day, he told him that the special team was being established, and that he had listed Andy as a consultant: "Mind you, you're not actually on the team since you may be involved, but we want you to be informed in case you have something to add.

"Now, how are you coming with Goodie Goods Import Export?"

"So far, nothing tangible, but I still feel that there's something wrong, if I can just figure it out. The paperwork is perfect, almost as though somebody made it up. Usually, there are minor mistakes, which are understandable, but this stuff seems too good to be true. I'm not ready yet to give them a clean bill of health."

"Well, keep plugging and don't let this hot weather fry your brain," said Tom as he left.

Two days later Andy sighed as he plunked himself down at his makeshift desk, which was covered with paper. He picked up a clump from the unsorted pile and looked at the papers with a puzzled frown. They were credits and debits between Goodie Goods main office in New Orleans and its branch office in Charleston. He thought they must have been included by accident, but he put them in order by date and began reading them.

The amounts listed were very small, insignificant really, and the profits involved would hardly pay for the paperwork. But the descriptions of the goods were unusually long and complex. He was more and more puzzled as he read them through. He stared at his sunflower, which had grown three feet since he had been immured. Then he phoned Tom.

"Tom, I've found something which I'd like you to see. Can you come by?"

When Tom arrived, Andy showed him the papers, pointing out the inconsistencies and the ways in which they differed from typical communications within a company.

"What do you think the significance is, Andy?"

"I'm wondering if it can be a cypher."

Tom paused a moment before he said, "OK. We'll get a cryptologist on the papers and have copies made for you. It certainly doesn't look normal. And just to be on the safe side, we'll ask the task force if Goodie Goods has turned up anywhere in their investigations."

Late that day Tom called Andy. Despite his usual noncommittal manner, he was excited.

"Andy, I think you've given us a break through. The task force found that an employee of Goodie Goods in New Orleans is someone whom they've been keeping an eye on because he's a member of one of the extreme racist groups that might have been involved in the Brewer killing. The cryptologist is champing at the bit. I'll keep in touch."

For the next few days, Andy continued sorting through blameless paperwork from Goodie Goods and watching the sunflower grow. Then he was called to attend a meeting at the local office.

As he entered the crowded room, he realized that it was a joint meeting including not only the local police and the FBI task force members, but also the district federal prosecutor, who called the meeting to order.

"Early this morning we made arrests in several states on charges of murder in the first degree and conspiracy to commit murder. There was a nation-wide plot to discourage and stop efforts being made by organizations, including VMR, to register voters before the upcoming elections. Although we were concerned about the situation, we had not been able to pick up any chatter on the internet nor had our inside sources been able to learn anything. Then an agent in this office found the means by which encrypted messages were being exchanged, and it was all laid out for us. I am calling a news conference this afternoon to make the public announcement.

"Off the record, I'd like to say there were two highly unusual coincidences which helped us break this case. Charles Brewer, a member of VMR, was killed almost under the nose of our agent who bore a remarkable resemblance to him, so we could not determine which man was the target. Therefore our agent continued his ongoing audit of Goodie Goods, where he found the encrypted messages. We have not determined yet whether Goodie Goods was taken advantage of by employees, or whether its officers were involved in the conspiracy. We will be continuing work in that area. That's all for today. Thank you."

Madonna

By Virginia Braxton

The life-size Madonna stood on the bed of the scavenger's truck amid old rebars, a refrigerator, and rusty iron fences. Her faded blue robe seemed too thin to keep her warm and she was very pale, but she was unconcerned by the junk surrounding her.

She had begun in the home of an old Latvian woman whom the scavenger's wife cared for. When the woman died, her children gave the Madonna to the scavenger's wife who managed to find room for her in their crowded apartment. The Madonna liked being there with all the people, but when the scavenger's mother-in-law moved in with them, there simply was not enough room. The Madonna was moved to the scavenger's truck.

The scavenger had no garage for his truck and worried about leaving the Madonna outside. He tried covering her with a tarpaulin at night, but the Madonna was claustrophobic. He needed to find her some kind of shelter.

He tried a convent first, but there he was told that as the Madonna could not lift her arms enough to help them serve the poor, she would have to go somewhere else. He took her to a store that sold second hand religious articles on consignment, but there he was told that the Madonna was not good enough art nor intrinsically valuable enough for them to handle. He tried taking her to a homeless shelter, but that shelter only took in men: the staff suggested a women's shelter they knew of. He tried it, but it was for abused women, and the Madonna did not qualify. Another shelter was only for people who were trying to get their lives back on track, and no one thought the Madonna had lost track of her life. At still another shelter, he was told that the Madonna was a religious symbol and the terms of their federal grant prohibited them from having any religious symbols in their shelter. So the Madonna continued to ride around among the scavenged materials.

One evening while driving along the underground expressway, which avoided the snarled streets at the surface, the scavenger saw an encampment of homeless people. He stopped, unloaded the Madonna, and shouted, "Here's a Madonna: She's homeless too!" Then he drove off.

Some days later, he was trying to use the underground expressway, but the traffic was terrible. It was start and stop but mostly stop. He called to a cabbie in the next lane and asked what the trouble was.

"It's the Underground Madonna!" the cabbie explained. "The homeless people have a miraculous Madonna and people are bringing her gifts. The

Mayor wants to move her but the homeless people have vowed to form a human shield to keep her with them." When traffic finally moved far enough, the scavenger saw that the homeless people had built his Madonna an altar-like shelter of sturdy cardboard. There were votive candles and piles of flowers in front of her.

The ACLU filed a suit on behalf of the Madonna and requested a court order to let the Madonna stay where she was.

The mayor was concerned about snarling traffic, but said he would work with the homeless coalition, which had pledged to find shelter for the Madonna where she was accessible to their clients, and he would work with other municipal departments, including the Transit Authority. In the meantime, the "Madonna of the Underground" could remain where she was.

After negotiations, the Transit Authority donated a bus shelter, which was then repurposed as a Madonna Shelter. The Madonna and her shelter were placed on a grassy area near an entrance to the underground expressway, with a sign over them, "The Underground Madonna." When he passed by, the scavenger saw a great pile of offerings at her feet, put there, he thought, by the people kneeling on the grass in front of the Madonna.

Hut Mates

By Virginia Braxton

Sven looked up as he felt a change in the Artic atmosphere and realized that he was in the path of serious weather. No time to get back to base camp, but he could see one of the emergency shelters which were scattered throughout the preserve. He thought he could make it there before the storm hit, and almost did. He staggered the last few yards and was relieved when the wind slammed him against the structure.

He was surprised to find the door partially open. He pushed it the rest of the way open and stepped in. He was greeted by a stench, and stubbed his toe against something where the floor should have been empty.

He chanced using his mini-light and found he was looking at a polar bear. It had been mauled and was dead, but not for long.

Sven stood thinking for a moment. He knew his own survival depended on his staying in the hut and there wasn't room for both him and the bear's carcass. He decided he would have to drag the body outside, so he lifted its head and began pulling. He had it partway through the door when the sound of the wind stopped for a moment and he heard a faint mewling. He shone his mini-light on the corpse and saw part of it moving, feebly, but moving. What hair he had stood on end. He looked more carefully and realized that it was a cub.

What an anomaly! It was nowhere near the birthing season, so this cub was premature.

How had it managed to survive its mother's death? If he put it out in the storm, it would certainly die, and, after all, he was a wildlife conservationist. He had to detach the cub from its mother so he could close the door and give him and it a chance to survive. He located the thermal blanket in the supply stash, but it rattled when he put it next to the cub who seemed to shrink away. Sighing, he unzipped his anorak and pulled off the fleece vest he had on underneath. He wrapped the vest around as much of the cub as he could reach and pulled. The cub whimpered, but he pulled it free, and wrapping it securely in the vest, put it next to his chest and rezipped his anorak.

He finally managed to drag the mother's carcass out of the hut and close the door. He wrapped himself in the thermal blanket and lay panting for a few moments. Exhausted and without meaning to, he fell asleep.

The bundle against his chest wiggled and mewed, waking him. Sighing, he wondered what in the hut could approximate bear milk. And he needed water and food himself. He heaved himself off the floor and noticed that it was oddly silent. He realized the wind was no longer howling.

He opened the door a crack and was blinded by the light. The squall had passed. Better yet, in the distance was the Wildlife Conservancy snowmobile. Propping himself against the doorframe, he waved wildly, and it headed toward him.

His teammate Kai jumped off the mobile shouting, "Thank God for the personnel tracker devices they make us wear," and threw his arms out for a big bear hug.

"Careful!" responded Sven, "Don't crush the small friend I have in here!" and he opened his jacket so Kai could see the cub.

Kai looked at the cub. "Sven, I would have said you were a wolf man, but in any case, let's get this little fellow where he can be properly cared for. Hop on behind me, and we'll go straight to base camp. It isn't far on the mobile."

Kent Humpal Stories

Clark's Story

By Kent Humpal

Clark didn't often eat lunch out of the office, but he had met with some old school friends and agreed to meet them at the up-stairs restaurant at Bloomingdales. Stepping onto the escalator, he looked over at the mirrored wall, checking himself for fallout, when he saw a familiar face he thought he might be wrong. That can't be Perry Blake! He died two years ago. He just looks like him—that smile is sure familiar.

A week later, waiting at the transit stop, he saw the man again exiting the elevator, and then walking over to the up-town train platform. God that looks like Perry, he thought. Even the loping walk was his. Hah, just looks like him, but it can't be. Police and coroner deposed the body. Even though he was burned, he had a medical ID bracelet and a charred wallet. There was no family to identify what was burned badly, so that closed the case.

That night he mentioned it to Flora. Perry had been at their anniversary and she had danced with him there and at company affairs. "Flora, do you remember Perry Blake from the company?"

"Sure I do—he was a good dancer. A little too handsy, if you let him be. Wasn't he the one that they investigated after his death?" she asked.

"Yeah, they found a lot of discrepancies with his accounts—the appropriation of funds, especially from his elderly clients. Some company funds and credit card accounts were overdue or misused also. The company had to reimburse several clients for thousands of dollars—probably hundreds of thousands. It was kept pretty much in house though."

"What about him?" Flora asked.

Clark replied, "I swear I saw him a week ago and then again today at the underground. If it's not him he must have a brother or a dopple-ganger."

"What's a dopple-ganger," said Flora.

"It's a complete look-alike—an identical person. Kind of like some of the celebrity doubles, but more exact. You know they say everyone has a duplicate somewhere in the world. It does make me curious though," Clark said thoughtfully.

He couldn't help himself, and his curiosity got the best of him. He stopped at the boss's office. "You recall the shock and dismay we felt after the Perry Blake episode, Mr. Thurray."

"I certainly do. We are still recovering from the discrediting of our reputation. The insurance company raised our rates and demanded increased background checks on all of our employees. It's been a black-mark on our family owned company."

"Well I know it seems impossible but I swear I saw Blake recently and more than once," Clark said. "Here in the financial district."

"Security was never happy with the investigation and neither was the insurance company. That's why the repayment was so slow. Why don't you talk to Ralph Sutton in Security."

Ralph was interested. "See what you can do about getting something that might identify this guy. I was never happy with the outcome."

A little over a week later, Clark spotted the man getting on the up-town train and followed him onto the car. He paid no specific attention to him but cautiously checked him out. His hair was lighter and the hair-cut was stylish but shorter. The short, white scar peeking out from his moustache was familiar. Perry said he got it in a rugby game. Clark got off and as he turned to the window, lifted his phone to his mouth and snapped several shots through the window, hoping to get a full-face of the man. Ralph was intrigued but said, although the photo convinced him, it wasn't enough to go to the insurance investigators.

This time he sat across from the person he was convinced was Perry Blake. "I've seen you on the train or in the transit system. Do you work around here? I work as an accountant for a firm near-by."

"I work as a private financial advisor. I'm on my own. I don't like working in a big firm. I can pick my own clients that way."

"I'm Clark Sutton, been with the same company almost 6 years now. A smaller family owned group."

"I'm Paul Blaine, been here about 7 months. I know I've seen you around. Enough to count you as a familiar face. Well, I get off here." and he left. Clark noticed it wasn't his usual stop.

Over the next month they saw each other several times. Clark smiled and gestured in a familiar manner but didn't sit by him. Clark ventured to the seat opposite Perry. They both were reading financial news but Clark took the opportunity to look closer but only briefly at the man he suspected was Perry Blake. Yes, the eyes were the same but a different shade than the eyes in the security files. One eye was slightly larger than the other. They're contacts to change the color. There was evidence around the eyes of a subtle lift or shape change. The easy smile, but better teeth. The new Paul Blaine caught him looking and turned toward the window. Clark looked at the reflection and there he saw the convincing evidence. There it was the Perry Blake smirky smile—the one that appeared when he convinced a client to enter a somewhat questionable investment. Over the next couple of weeks, Clark collected a juice bottle, a Starbucks cup, and a couple of cigarette butts, which he gave to Ralph in Security.

Two months later, in the papers and on the news, a story appeared. Perry Blake, known now as Paul Blaine, was arrested and indicted under several charges, including fraud, embezzlement, financial elder abuse, and insurance fraud. Further investigation was undergoing concerning the death of the person previously identified in the scorched ear.

The police and the insurance company lauded and praised a private citizen for his awareness and help in obtaining this arrest. At his behalf, they are keeping his identity unknown. The insurance company has awarded him 10% of the funds recovered. The amount was unreleased.

Clark began to think about what he had learned from this event. If his wife went along with the idea. He made a list:

1. Wife separate/move out of state/re-marry later.
2. Have no children/close relatives.
3. Never, never return to the old home.
4. Be more alert to physical changes.
5. Change occupation.

You know, I bet I could get away with it!

Thanksgiving 1945

By Kent Humpal

In the years during WWII my family lived in a very small house in Mountain View, California. It had no refrigerator, only a small gas heater, and the bathtub was in a curtained off room off the washroom. The bathtub was filled by carrying buckets of water from the adjoining laundry tub in the porch.

The kitchen stove was an old porcelain model with 3 top burners and a very small oven. It used natural gas with no pilot light, so it had to be lit with a wooden match.

Turkeys were being hard to obtain during this time, since specialty foods were being shipped to the armed forces, in most cases, so the prospect of having an actual turkey for Thanksgiving was dim.

About this time my mother's youngest sister had moved from Washington DC to San Jose, where she found work with the Food Machinery Corp. known locally as FMC. She lived in the San Jose YWCA, as most rooms were for young, unmarried women,

As the war wound down, many commodities of food, including turkeys, were released to the civilian population. As a result, the employees of FMC, as a bonus, were given certificates for a turkey. My aunt Wanda, having only our family as relatives in

Northern California, decided that we should collect the turkey and share it with my grandmother, who just moved here from Nebraska. My father's uncle, aunt and cousin, also lived just across the street from us in Mountain View, as they would love eating some turkey.

The day arrived to pick up the turkey, so we all got into the family car, drove to San Jose, picked up my aunt at the YWCA, and proceeded to a large warehouse near the train tracks on the outer edge of San Jose. My father and aunt went to the door on the loading platform. They pressed a bell and a man came out and they explained the situation and handed him the certificate.

The agent looking down at us in the car may have made a judgement, or it may just have been the luck of the draw when he went to get the turkey. He may have seen us as the Cratchet family, with Tiny Tim, for he came out with largest turkey, solidly frozen, that I have ever seen. It dwarfed the turkeys in the windows of Harry's Hofbrau and Boston Market.

Arriving back at our small house, my mother faced the fact that it would not fit in her miniscule oven. It turned out to be a 32lb block of frozen turkey. So it would sit in the back porch laundry tub for 7 days thawing out before it could even be cooked.

Finally, my great uncle Roland came over with a saw and cut it in half. Even half of it barely fit in the oven. Eventually, cooking half in my uncle's house and half in ours we were able to get the turkey baked for Thanksgiving dinner.

We ate turkey for what seemed to be days. It was truly a Thanksgiving, because my youngest uncle and several cousins would be returning from the war. As for the turkey, my uncle Roland remarked that "Even the gravy was tough" for to have attained that size he must have lived to a ripe old age and may well have passed on from old age.

Keeping a Secret

By Kent Humpal

I moved across the Hallway to Howie standing by his locker. I sidled up close to him and said in a low voice. "Howie can you keep a secret?" He was a close friend, one of only a handful of kids my age that lived in our mostly orchard neighborhood. We met on the school bus and it turned out we were in the same 4th grade Class at Highway Elementary.

"Sure, what's it about? Something good or bad?" he asked.

"Well, the prom is coming up in 3 weeks and you know that I am going with Camille Peirvicci. Her family is catholic and you and Rosey Renoldi have been going together for several months. Would you double date with us? It might cool things for us, so please ask Rosey and let me know at the end of school."

We went our separate ways, and we had no classes together but still saw each other on campus. At lunch he walked over from his usual crowd. As we moved away from my semi-jock group, Howie said," I told Rosey what you said and she was going to talk to Cammie about it. There should be no problem. You know my family being Croatian has not been too popular with Rosey's Italian parents either but we go to the same church and our moms are in the same ladies' groups.

The next week went by with the prom being set up. Howie would drive. He and Rosey would be with me when we picked up Cammie. After dinner, we would go to the prom and mingle with our own groups. Prom week had arrived. Tuxes were rented, corsages ordered, cars washed and cleaned. No limos in our crowds. Rumors spread about secret rooms rented, break-ups, hair-do and dress problems. Word went around that Howie and Rosey had broken up and Cammie was the cause. Howie assured me there was no reason to worry. Cammie said there was no cause to be upset. Rosey and Cammie were still talking, so what could be the problem.

During 5th period English Dolores, the boss gossip and newsletter leaned over to me and said," Ronnie, can you keep a secret? It's about Howie and Camille."

Quilty
By Kent Humpal

My friend, Red, was born and raised around Lake Almaner. If you are not aware of this lake, it is on the headwater of the Feather River, or El Rio del Plumas, which was named for the white feather-like ripples and rapids on the river, before it was tamed by the numerous small dams all erected by PG&E.

Red, as his friends called him, had many adventures and tales of growing up in Chester CA. Before the railroad came along, I believe the Chester & the McLeod were floating logs down the river, but by the 1930's the logs were mostly trucked in.

Logging and Sawmills were principle employers at that time and small towns like Chester, Greenville, Westwood, Shasta City and McLeod were thriving. Now they are being saved from being "Ghost Towns" by the tourist trade. Company towns of family homes and dormitories are now second homes and rentals.

Nevertheless, I digress. Red was now the Art Teacher in the county seat of Lassen County—one of a few born and raised in the area. Most of us were younger and just starting our careers.

About his pet, I'll just call it Quilty—I do not know if he really had a name. Red was a hunter and that part of CA is isolated and wild country. Red and a friend were deer hunting, or at least scouting around for likely spots. I would not say he was a stickler for the rules. Anyway, he and a friend were out around Lee's Meadows near Warner Creek looking for likely deer signs and habitats. As they moved near the creek looking over crushed grass, hoof prints, and other signs, they also kept watch for Black bears, checking for scratch marks on trees trampled berry patches and ripped logs.

Red mentioned that the bears rarely were dangerous, but you particularly had to watch for mama or other filling up before hibernation. Moving through the brush and forest they became aware of a high-pitched whimpering and chirping sound. It was not in the brush or on the ground. Finally looking up, Red and his friend saw a very young Porcupine huddled on the top of a tree limb. Looking around for a parent, but seeing or hearing nothing they continued on their scout.

An hour or so later, working back toward their track, they came upon the little "Porky" still in the tree, no parent visible or calling. Red, being a mountain boy, now man, decided to take him home to Chester. His home was in the woods so he didn't think about any problems and the local Rangers were all friends. Wild or partly tamed pets were not uncommon in the area if they didn't cause a problem, or if nobody mentioned it. Quilty went home and became a family pet.

Red said he never became cuddly but he followed the family members around the yard. Quilty and the family dogs and cat came to a mutual understanding—tolerant, but not buddies. Tourists found it intriguing to see Quilty following the family around, occasionally riding on a shoulder or in a wheel barrow. He lived with them for several years and then he was gone. They never knew whether he went looking for a mate but hoped he hadn't run into another wild animal that knew how to handle Porcupines.

Red said the only problems they had with Quilty was that he had a strong need to gnaw on items. Of course, he liked bark and foliage but he also liked the handles of shovels, rakes, any wood equipment, especially if it had residue of sweaty salt from a person's hands. Leather gloves were a delicacy to be chewed up quickly if used and sweaty.

The family soon learned to put things away as did nearby neighbors. Tennis rackets, baseball bats, and gloves were fair game. Quilty waddled along without undue attention from the locals, several of whom had deer, wild ducks, geese and according to Red, a Bobcat raised from a kitten. Quilty went on his own call of the wild.

Goldie Lox and The Three Bears

By Kent Humpal

Setting: Late Spring in Northern California, in the Santa Cruz Area.

Maizle Korn, known as Goldie, and her parents "Pop" and Sweta, had been arguing for several days. Pop and Sweta wanted her to go with them to visit her grandparents in the Santa Cruz area and she was resisting. Goldie agreed to go when her best friends, Ida Ho, Wilda Ness, and Bessie Mae Mucho were allowed to go along too. The grandparents, Colonel and Carmela Korn, lived near one of the small towns near Roaring Camp, and the girls thought they could sneak off and take the train to the beach and boardwalk for most of the day.

Goldie, having grown bored with the beach and boardwalk talk, decided to hitchhike to UCSC to mingle with the University crowd. Dropped off by tourists near a side road, she was never sure if it was Bean Hollow or Old Felton Road.

Goldie began walking on a small trail she thought would take her to the USCS campus. After several minutes of hiking, Goldie, unprepared as usual, became hot, thirsty, and tired. While sitting down, unhappy at her circumstances, she spots a clearing in the forest with a small, rustic home set back in the trees. Her cell phone was of no use among the redwoods so it sends Goldie scurrying up the path to see if the folks have a landline to call her friends or parents.

When no one answers her knocking or cell phone calls, and only a screen door exists between her and the living room, without any hesitation Goldie enters the home. Seeking refreshments, water or whatever she can find, she opens the refrigerator. Taking note of the cards and messages on the refrigerator door she realizes ironically that she is in the house of the three Bears—Bruno, Griselda, and Theodore.

Sorting over the shelves, Goldie comes out with bagels, lox, cream goat, and Kefir Cheeses. Looking for something to wash down the food, Goldie spots several bottles of home labeled beer in the back. Grabbing the first bottle, Goldie wanders over and sets in the large, heavy lounge chair. Discovering the beer is as dark and heavy as the chair, after a couple of sips, she leaves it on the counter and grabs a bottle with a different label. Settling in the smaller platform rocker she leans back with purloined goodies with the second bottle.

Taking a big swallow, she realizes this one is so light and pale that it is almost tasteless. Sighing and disappointed as only one of the elite can be, Goldie goes for the next bottle. Going to the medium sized recliner, she finds she is sipping down a copper colored amber brew that just fits her personality. This is the beer for the entitled, namely for me. Weary and dozing off she turns on the afternoon talk show and then falls asleep.

Returning home from a foraging excursion, the Bears discover Goldie dozing off in their living room. Bruno, seeing the spilled beer and cheese on the arm of his favorite chair, lets out a low growl. Griselda, seeing the wet ring on her side table, laments the lack of a coaster and glowers at the warm open bottle. Only Ted, seeing the irony of the situation calls out, "Well, it finished the last bottle of Teddy Bears Amber Ale and there. It now sleeps on my recliners."

By the time the deputies leave, having sorted out the situation, Goldie, the Bears and Parents are all accounted for and present. Goldie's misdemeanors of knocking, entering, and underage drinking are withdrawn by the Baer's refusal to press charges, as it seems the Baer's had come from Tahoe to escape tourists and were themselves using the cabin without authorization.

They thought, rightly, that no one would notice in Santa Cruz, or care if they did notice. Between their craft brews and pot cultivation, no one wanted to turn them in. Although charged with out of season salmon and steak fishing, the charges were dropped with the court rulings that as native Californians they had prior legal rights.

When it turned out that Goldie was older than her parents claimed, Goldie became the spoke person and Rep in Northern California for Baers. The Baers, now known by their real names of Bear, sold out to Coors and moved to Wise River Montana.

Apple of My Ire
By Kent Humpal

Pretend that you are hungry and have been given an Artichoke to eat, and further assume that you are the very first person to eat an Artichoke. Write a short story about how you would approach such a situation.

On day 5, Eve and I have been out of Eden for a long period, so we are starving. Damn the apple—I wish I had it, for we are so hungry we could even eat the con-artist serpent, if he was here.

We have come upon a bunch of strange plants. Our guide, Michael, told us that they were edible and he called them Arty-chokes. He ate them and called them something like that. He has a strange sense of humor however.

Eve and I took a couple of them but were not able to figure out how to eat them. We tried eating them the way we ate the apple and learned that it couldn't be done. When we got fire, we tried roasting them, but they just got dry and scorched and became very tough.

We could hear chuckling coming from the clouds above and a clay tablet with directions almost hit us in the head. It told us to boil them, whatever that means, in a white pot. Avoiding the sticky points on the things, we split a couple with sharp stones and slow boiled them in the coals from the fire. The ever-helpful Michael's instructions said to use butter or olive oil on them as they are being boiled.

Have you ever tried squeezing an olive? After being bruised severely by an Aurox and a couple of Wild Goats, we finally got some thick liquid onto the artichokes. After several experimental attempts at eating them, we gave up. We are thinking now about roasted serpent baked with apple slices. I will keep you up to date, as soon as we find some more clay for a tablet. Eve has begun calling them apple for some reason, even saying it was a Macintosh. I said NO way.

Sincerely,
Adam

An American Family History

By Kent Humpal

She was in her early fifties and had become interested in family and ancestry. Although some of it was for her children's sake, mostly it was curiosity. Her parents, now in their seventies, rarely talked about family, especially ancestors beyond their parents. From pictures and family stories when aunts and uncles came for the Holidays, she knew they were Norwegian and English for the most part, but no stories of migration had settled in or no hardships. Not even when they came to the U.S.

Like her, her husband had been an only child and he only outlived his parents by a few years. She knew his family came to the U.S. as children in the early 1920's from Scotland and Northern England and there were stories from uncles and cousins of family, some still over in the British Isles. However, she knew nothing about her own family. In fact, they seemed to shut down whenever she was there.

One day while watching PBS, **Who Do You Think You Are** came on, and she was fascinated by the researchers and how they found information on people—even events and facts that had been lost or hidden for a generation or two. At the end of the show, when the site for DNA popped up, she jotted it down. A few days later, coming across her scribbled note, she went to her computer, brought up the site, and sent for a kit. A week or so later the kit arrived, and after much work she dutifully used the two swabs, sealed them carefully in the containers, and mailed them into the Ancestry.

Two weeks, then three weeks went by and then as she opened the front door after work she saw the thick envelope on the doorstep. Picking it up, she tossed it onto the side table thinking here was another advertising brochure, and she went into the kitchen, checked the phone for calls, and poured an iced tea.

Neither her son or daughter had called nor was there a message from her parents. Thinking about dinner, she walked back into the living room and picked up the manila envelope. Reading the return address and seeing the Ancestry logo, excitedly she opened the flap. Quickly skimming the explanatory material, she went right to the pie graph to see what it said. She stared at it, bewildered by what she saw and by the percentages in each section. As she had expected, it was over 70% North European, but surprisingly to her mostly it was French and Scots, with a small percentage of Dutch. The fourth wedge of the pie made her sit down, gasping, and trying to take in what it meant. It had to be an error, a screw up by the DNA lab. The fourth block stated that she was 28% American Indian. How could it be? Her parents were 2nd generation. They came from small close-by towns. Everyone knew everyone else and there would have been gossip.

She thought and wondered about it for the next month, mentioning it to no one. She re-read the material with the kit. It not only said American Indian but narrowed it down to a particular tribe, the Winnebago. She knew little about Native Americans and weren't Winnebago's motor homes and campers?

For the next several weeks, she spent her free time on the internet and the library researching the Winnebagos. They were one of the Peoples of the Lakes, surrounded by larger, more powerful tribes. Displaced by and often submerged into other groups, eventually American settlers took over their lands and they almost disappeared. Now they were a very small band of a few families intermarried with other tribes and often they were white as much as Indian. Although many had long ago integrated, a few lived on a small reservation with the Sauk and Fox tribes.

With all the tribal information she had gathered, she still knew nothing about her own situation. She didn't want to confront her parents; she loved them very much and they had given her a good life. Her children didn't have to know yet. She would figure it out.

Contacting a few agencies that helped locate birth parents and adopted children, a much easier and accepted practice at present, she located a private investigator that specialized in that type of investigation and was considered not only honest but discreet. Giving him all the information she had; birth date; location; certification from a doctor and nurse; and the DNA results, she left it up to the detective agency.

Several weeks and some months passed. There had only been brief statements, but no face-to-face meetings with the detective, and she was getting anxious. Besides fees were beginnings to add up. Sitting at her desk in the real estate office, she checked phone messages and there it was—a call from the agency to please give them a return call at her convenience. Setting up a meeting was her first priority, so she made the call right then.

Setting in the agencies office, she waited with both hopefulness and trepidation. What had they found out? Why had she been given up? Why the secrecy? The agent stepped in carrying a folder full of papers. Giving her some time to compose herself, he began laying out some papers. Then he began to speak.

"I'm sorry it took us so long, but the information was pretty much false. First, you were born about two weeks earlier than your birth certificate states, in a small town near the Winnebago community in

Michigan, actually not far from here. We have located an uncle who lives near there presently. He provided us with really pertinent information. He was and is a friend of your family and a principle in your rather unique situation. After I contacted him, he and your parents met and would like to meet with you to tell you what happened. They suggest you bring their grandchildren to the meeting.

Two weeks later, they all met in her parents' home. She knew everyone but the man talking to her parents. He was lean, athletic looking, about her parents age with only a hint of Indian in his features. In fact he was blue-eyed and about her complexion. Her children had left their kids at home, so there were only adults in the room.

"I am a member of an agency that specializes in reacquainting birth parents and their children and vice-verse. We only work with the consent of both parties to avoid problems. This was one of the more interesting cases and luckily, everyone was positive and agreeable. Let me introduce you to Mr. William Littleton. This is your mother's brother, your blood uncle. You will want to hear his story."

"Hello niece, let's get on with the story of your mother and your birth. Your mother was two years younger than I was. It was the early 60's and although the Civil Rights and race movements were going on it didn't touch us up here very much—besides we were Indian or part Indian and not black.

"We grew up in a predominantly white community and blended in pretty well, at least your mother and I did. It was easier for me, as a boy and being athletic, I fit right in. I played Lacrosse, ran track, and was good enough to get a scholarship to a small college. It was tougher for your mother. She was pretty, maybe a little exotic looking. Now days she could be a newscaster, or work as a sales agent.

"She attracted the attention of everyone and began hanging out with the wrong crowd. Kind of like "Grease" with a bad ending. Rumors began circulating about "hot" Indian girls getting her drunk. By the time she was 18 she was an alcoholic and our parents couldn't control her. I came home from college when I was 22 and became reacquainted with your parents. By then my sister was pretty far gone being alcoholic, living wherever she could, with little chance at recovery and also being pregnant."

Her father continued the narration. "Your mother and I had been married three years and found out we couldn't have children. It would be different now, but not then. When William told us about his sister and her situation we thought about it and then came up with a solution. We would move out of the area for a long enough time to make sure your age was reasonable. We had friends who could help with documents. William, listening to this broke in, "my sister was in very bad shape. Her alcoholism and wild living had left her with kidney problems and liver problems. She was only lucid and communicative occasionally. I talked to her but she wasn't aware of the severity of her problems. The tribe was no help, for they would have insisted on custody of the baby and I couldn't take care of a baby."

"I was working as a carpenter and trying to get a contractor license. When your parents came to me with their idea I saw it as an ideal solution. Her father spoke up, "we moved out of state and I got a transfer from the company. We knew the approximate date of your birth so set up a reasonable length of time and let friends and family think your mom was pregnant."

Her uncle went on. "Your mother agreed it was the best thing to do for you so it really wasn't a kidnapping as such, but was more a rescue. A woman from the reservation helped with the birth a few months after your parents moved.

"Your birth mom was in and out of it, but she saw you and gave her blessing. Two days later, I took you away and gave you to your parents. Your mother only lived a few months after your birth. In and out of conscientious, I took care of her at home. She's buried in the local cemetery if you want to visit her grave, Yvonne Littleton, age 20. Her Indian name is also there, **Full Moon Lighting the Dark** is its English translation. For the first, time her mother talked.

"We wanted a child so badly and you were so beautiful. Somehow, you were healthy without complications from your mother's alcoholism, probably due to your uncle's care. We don't know anything about your father. I doubt if we ever will. We know that we always loved you, you were ours and are still."

The son and daughter sat there dumb founded. This was not what they had been expecting. "What does this mean about us? I don't know what to think. What are we and our kids? You are our grandchildren and great grandchildren. You were before this news and always will be. We love you like we love your mom, you are our family no matter what DNA says.

"Let's fill in some newer information," said their newly discovered uncle. "I have followed your life, after all you are my niece. You might have noticed me at school events, your wedding, birthdays, etc. I own a home construction and remodeling business. One of your cousins works with me, the other is an architect in the city. You have several nieces and nephews living nearby. We would love to get to know your family. We've stayed away to keep you from any embarrassment or legal problems, but that's over now depending on how you accept this situation."

Still trying to absorb the information while looking at everyone she replied, "I was looking for reasons which I was stolen, abandoned, or unloved. That's all been explained now and nothing really changed. I love my parents, they gave me a good life. My children and grandchildren haven't changed and they love their grandparents. Why would I reject them? Let's keep it in the family archives for future generations."

The spokesmen for the agency spoke up, "you may want to know there are a few benefits to your Indian ancestry. Your uncle didnt mention it, but although the Winnebago tribe is very small and dispersed the US government recognizes it and therefore you are members, as as soon as you register with the government and show proof. The DNA test will do that. You and your children as well as your grandchildren will get a few tax breaks, even tuition grants if qualified for educational reduction. Now the legal tribe may not accept you but Uncle Sam does. Think it over, goodbye, its been an interesting and satisfactory case."

Elvet Moore Stories

The Lonely Ghost
By Elvet Moore

In the town of Charlottesville, South Carolina, an old homestead had stood for several decades, which was the oldest property in town. It had been over ten years since anyone had occupied the home, so it did not take long for the town's people to soon believe that there was an old ghost occupying the home, even though none had ever been seen, as yet.

Inside the home, there was the usual old furniture with webs of white dust and powder connected from every arm or leg. Ten years ago when the last person occupied the home, the owner caught a bit of the flu and ended up going to the town doctor, who placed him into a rest home under quarantine. Soon thereafter he passed away, and ever since then the old home has been empty, with the local bank holding the paper on it, hoping someone would come forward to want to live in the home. With the above as a background, I began my journey into living in the old city of Charlottesville, along with a ghost or two.

My name is Charles Swanson, and I am now 70 years old. My wife passed away last year, and we do not have any children, so I found myself very lonely. I soon found out that there was a city in the USA that offered a home to be managed and fixed up from scratch, so I decided to go and take a look at the homestead myself. It was located in Charlottesville, South Carolina, USA.

When I arrived in the city, I proceeded directly to the bank where I found out details about 567 North Plains Boulevard, which had been empty for about ten years. The price for the home was about half the price of other homes of that age, which had not sunk into such a deep state of repair, so the obvious deal was to buy the home and spend a number of years fixing it up before selling it again, if I wanted to do so. Since I was alone and lonely, it seemed to me that working on this home would be just what I needed to do in order to find a more relaxed state of mind.

The bank mortgage fellow was very pleased to show me the home. Together we parked in front of it.

The yard around the home had been kept up so the home would seem to be okay, but beyond the grass and shrubs was a home that needed fixing up for sure. Some of the wood was rotten, and the paint was chipped off from what was left of the wood.

"Mr. Swanson, let's go into the home through the door on the right hand side of the porch," the mortgage fellow said, for he knew the front door was loose on its hinges.

"That's fine with me," I said.

In a couple of minutes, we were both inside. Aside from the obvious white dust and powder stretching from furniture arm to furniture leg, the home seemed to be carefully laid out. The furniture was a rather nice mixture of dark oak and light brown trim, so I figured it wouldn't take me long to get the house fixed up to look like something.

There was a second and third floor, and there was nice furniture at each landing and in each room. After spending a couple of hours I followed the mortgage fellow to the basement, where it appeared there would be only a black hole dug into the dirt. However, an old furnace was still there and it looked like it had not been operated for several years.

After spending a number of hours examining the home, the mortgage fellow and I went back to his office and we sat down to negotiate the price. On the market it was listed as $98K, which was about half the price for similar homes. I decided I could offer a bit less, however, since no one had wanted the home for all of these years. Hence, after much haggling, I walked away with a price of $89K, and I was able to pay cash. I now own the old home, and as soon as I fix up the upstairs bedroom, I will have a place to hang my hat and other laundry items.

While fixing up the old place, I stayed in the town motel. It took me four weeks to fix things up, so afterwards I moved into the bedroom at the top of the stairs, and I was now in my own home sweet home. In the meanwhile, there was an old friendly ghost living in the home. He usually stayed in the basement; for the darkness there afforded him the opportunity to sleep when he wanted, or just hang out and read some material he had that was bright enough for him to see.

The ghost recognized my work to be aimed at fixing up the home and realized that in time he would have to come out of the basement and seek a better life living near me. He did not plan to scare me, however. He just wanted a friend like me to be with him whenever he sought friendship.

One night when I went to bed in the old bed upstairs, I was awakened by the sound of someone or something walking around the home. I quickly got out of bed and put on my slippers and walked down the stairs. To my surprise, the old ghost was sitting in one of the large chairs in the living room reading his book.

He looked up and said to me, "Hello, I'm living here, and I don't plan to scare you. Where are you living?"

"I usually hang out in the old bedroom at the head of the stairs. Have you been watching me all of this time while I fixed up the house?"

"I do get to see everything, but I didn't have any plan to scare you. Yes, I watched you, but I kept in the background."

The old ghost sat on the edge of my bed and fascinated me with the tales he told me. He had been born an ordinary person in 1800, and having died a horrible death in 1820, he decided to play ghost ever since.

I asked him how is it that some persons who die end up being a ghost while others do not act ghostlike at all. He wasn't sure but he said that he knew some ghost friends who could probably discuss the matter with a bit of reality, so he planned to take me to where they were.

After spending a few more weeks fixing up the home, I found myself living in all the rooms with my ghost friend, who watched me, but who didn't bother me. Some other ghosts arrived in the basement of the home, but when we wanted them to leave they were willing to go immediately, jumping ship without trying to scare anyone.

I am now over 90 years old and I definitely do believe in ghosts. I wondered, however, if that would be the case if the ghosts in the old home had been the scary kind.

Amends

By Elvet Moore

Susie Brown left her home on Monday morning to see if she could find work in the school library. She had already applied for the job, but she didn't know if there would be several other girls applying for the same position, and she wasn't sure whether she was fit for the job anyway.

At 7:45 am she walked into the Main Library Office and sat down to see what was going to happen. While waiting there she found out that there were nine other girls coming in and she assumed that they were all applying for the same position she had applied for.

In order to get the job, she had already decided she would cheat a little and claim she had held the position before, for who knows what some of the other girls might have done before. However, she obviously didn't want to come in second or third and not get the position she really wanted.

During the morning, each girl was interviewed. Her name was number eight on the roster, so when it was her turn, she had worked up a story about how she was clearly the best candidate, even though her skills were just barely acceptable.

At the end of the process, six of the girls were not very skilled so they were told to look elsewhere. The four remaining included me and we were going to be further interviewed for the position.

As my turn came up, I began to panic somewhat for I didn't know exactly what I had told the interviewer before, and I didn't want to stretch the truth too far. However I had remembered enough to make my interview go pretty well and I actually came out first, for the other three girls had been told to go home, which left me as the possible winner.

I was told to come back to the library tomorrow morning to start the new job. I was to report to Mr. Adams who had done some work in my position prior to hiring someone. I hoped that he would be so busy that he would not know how to judge my capability, which was clearly quite low for the position.

The next morning I showed up early and found out that she and Mr. Adams were alone in the office. He was sitting reading about me when I arrived.

"Hello, Susie" he said to me. "You surely seem to fill the position quite well, according to this write up. Will you please take a seat by your computer and do what is called for on line one. I want to see how well you accomplish that."

At this moment, I really panicked, for I didn't have a clue how to perform the work. I sat first on my right side and then on my left side, trying to take up some time and see if I could fake it. Finally, I stood up and asked to go to the bathroom. I then grabbed my stuff, scooted out the door, and ran down the hall to the outside door.

Once I was outside, I realized that I should not have acted as if I knew everything. I realized that it was a mistake for me to claim a capability that I really didn't have. I decided to not act as if I knew it all from then on.

Chuck Northup Stories

Harry Ferret

By Chuck Northup

I work in Chicago in the city planning office, a large room on the 18th floor of a skyscraper, along with about forty other workers. A few months ago, a man joined our group, and we have made friends and go to lunch together most days. Bertram speaks English with a definite British accent that is difficult to understand at times—especially when he attempts to speak while eating. He still prefers tea during breaks and lunch, and as I've recently found out, at breakfast and dinner. I would call him a teetotaler, but he does drink beer, a drink that is extremely popular with Brits. In fact, he told me that beer bars are springing up all over England with the advent of microbreweries and bars selling artisan brews.

He comes from Peterborough in the east of England, which is mostly agricultural, but the area is somewhat depressed. He wanted something better, so he came to America to go to college and find work as a desk jockey to get away from farming.

He attended the University of Chicago, obtaining a degree in Business Administration, and he ended up with his first job here in the planning department. That was not all he obtained at college—he found the right girl, and they married as soon as they graduated.

My wife and I had recently moved to Chicago, and we were in need of friends. She confessed to me the other day that we should join some club or social group where we can meet others and make friends. I told her that I could do my share by making more friends at work—thus this growth of relationship with Bertram.

"Elliot," he said to me one day at lunch, "My wife and I would like to invite you to supper. Do you think you would be free this weekend, say Saturday?"

"You said supper; how does that differ from dinner?" I asked.

"Dinner is more formal. We Brits make a distinction, but either one is served around seven in the evening. Please come earlier to have a drink and tour the house."

"I can tell you right now that we're free on Saturday and I would be happy to join you for supper. Thank you. I'll need your address and maybe your phone number if we get lost."

"Good! Now remember this is supper—it is not formal, so just come in relaxed, comfortable clothing—no tie!

We found their home easily, a tract house that looked like most of the others nearby in a modest area. As we left the car, we could see that there was a large back yard with secure wire fencing all around that set it off from the other homes. We arrived about a half-hour early to share a drink before eating.

We rang the bell, and both Bertram and his wife came to the door. They ushered us in, and introductions were made to his wife, Nancy and my wife Beverly.

"Would you care for a drink? I'm not familiar with the bourbon you like, so I bought a bottle the shop suggested," said Bertram.

With that, he offered us a glass each of Four Roses, a Kentucky Straight Bourbon that I could never afford. Bertram continued, "I hope this bourbon will be OK. I've taught Nancy to drink beer, so we'll stick to that if you please."

I assured Bertram, "This Bourbon is better than what I usually buy. This will be quite a treat for us."

We sat and talked for a while and Nancy said," Would you like a grand tour of the house? It's so small that it takes only two minutes—bring your drinks with you."

She walked us from the living room, through the dining room where she had set a table for four, into the kitchen, where something with a delightful aroma was cooking, past a small back porch, then to the master bedroom.

"This next bedroom is Harry's," she announced.

"Harry?" I probed, "You never told me you had children. I didn't know you had a son."

"We don't," answered Bertram. "Nancy is speaking of Harry Ferret. He lives here with us."

"Oh!" I inhaled, "You have a boarder."

"We-ll—not a *paying* boarder," Nancy said as she opened the door.

Before us was not a bedroom at all because it contained no bed. Instead, there was a very large cage consisting of three stories with ladders to get to each, and a cubby hole from which protruded a little nose.

Nancy called out, "Harry, come out and meet some friends."

Out came a small furry animal with a long furry tail. Its body was black and white and the fur formed a mask around its eyes like thieves wear. Including its tail, it was about a foot-and-a-half long. It came out the hole and started jumping sideways with all fours.

"Folks," declared Bertram, "Meet Harry Ferret. He's a domesticated ferret that we keep as a pet. When no one else is around, we let him out of his cage, and he has the run of the house. He loves to get under things, and he's very mischievous, and collects small objects to make a pile. I've taught him a few tricks, such as, sit up and roll over. We let him out into the back yard every day with a leash and supervision so he doesn't dig his way out. That other cage is his food—live mice. He's hungry all the time, and his constitution is such that we must feed him often, so we have to keep buying feeder mice."

"Speaking of feeding, our food is ready. Please, let's all go to the table," said Nancy.

As we ate, Bertram told us more about ferrets. "Where I come from in England, there are lots of farms, and rabbits. The farmers hate the rabbits because they destroy their crops. England allows us to have ferrets to keep down the rodents. The ferrets go right down into the rabbit burrows and eat them. They also catch moles, gophers, rats, and mice, so ferrets are really good for agricultural land.

"In olden days, and I mean w-a-a-y back over 2,000 years ago, they were used by hunters. The hunter would muzzle his ferret, and it would go into a rabbit burrow and scare the rabbit out into a trap that the hunter was holding. It was that long ago that ferrets were domesticated. Today ferrets are not used much by hunters, but farmers use them a lot. Many countries even import them.

"The word ferret is interesting. The Latin equivalent from where it comes, means thief. No one knows whether the name came from the mask-like coloring over his eyes or the mischievous way that he takes things."

We finished off our dinner, which seemed British: Fish and Chips with a dessert of Figgie Pudding. We also had tea, of course. Nancy comes from a small town in Indiana and knows nothing about English food except what Bertram teaches her. She did a wonderful job of cooking tonight, and we told her so.

We stayed only about an hour longer and left with great feelings of finding new friends.

A Long Fall

By Chuck Northup

Have you ever wondered as you stood on the glass-bottomed Skywalk that protrudes out over the Grand Canyon, how many people or animals have dropped over the edge to fall one mile to the bottom?

Many have wondered, but no one can possibly answer that question. The canyon has been in existence for at least 10,000 years—long before humans were about. Human history does stretch back over 4,000 years in that area, and the first tribes who populated the canyon and its surroundings have a legend that they seldom relate for fear of reprisal.

I flew down into the canyon by helicopter to the village of Supai where the Havasupai have lived forever, but now their village, even though rebuilt several times, is still nothing more than a collection of adobe huts.

I spoke with a very old native whose family goes back several thousand years, and he told me a legend as we sat in the shade of an old adobe building in the extremely concentrated heat of the canyon floor. He said he did not fear reprisal because he does not believe the tale.

It seems there was a Chua—a native word for dragon—that roamed the flat plains surrounding the canyon. It didn't bother the lives of the people who lived in the canyon, but if they climbed to the top of the rim, there was always the danger they could be attacked and eaten by the Chua.

This Chua roamed an area of hundreds of miles. It was a fearsome creature in the form of a huge lizard that looked similar to the familiar, thin, small horned-toad that populated the desert--but hundreds of times larger. It had a blunt nose, two horns that stood up from the back of its head; its body was covered with scales with a row of sharp points running he length of its body to the end of its tail. It was brown and white, but its eyes were fiery, and its four legs had claws on all toes. Its length was about ten braces, a brace being the length of both arms outstretched, or about the length of a blue whale when the Chua's tail extended out behind it.

The natives saw it only occasionally because they did not go to the top of the canyon often. They were positive of only one Chua, but they feared there were several more in distant locations. The Chua was on the south rim of the canyon, but the natives felt that there were more on the north rim.

Hunting parties would go up to the south rim to locate deer or other animals for food. It seemed that every time they returned home, there was one less hunter. They were never sure how that hunter disappeared, but they thought it was through the wrath of the Chua. On one trip, the son of the chief disappeared, and because that was such an important act, the hunters decide that they would search for the Chu and kill it in retaliation.

They gathered together their bravest hunters and climbed out of the canyon. They didn't know where to search, so they started looking for the huge droppings that the Chua left behind. They soon came across what appeared to be a fresh pile of dung and knew they must be near the monster. The hunters fanned out in order to cover more territory and to ensure their safety. One hunter found a rough trail apparently made by the Chua dragging its tail on the ground. The hunter called out to the others, and they concentrated their hunt on this trail, following it until they saw the Chua.

It was far distant, standing on all fours, chewing on something they couldn't discern. The leader, realizing their small group was no match against this giant, formulated a plan to encircle the monster and drive it into the canyon.

The leader quietly signaled for the others to encircle the Chua and close in on it slowly. If they did this, they could force the Chua to submit, but the Chua had other thoughts.

It lashed out to the hunters who came close. Its breath was hot, forcing the hunters to retreat. But their leader directed the hunters in the rear to advance whenever the monster attacked, and poke the monster with their spears in the rear to distract it from attacking other hunters. This action kept the Chua busy turning about.

The hunters had only two weapons. Bows and arrows had not yet been conceived, but they had spears with sharpened points, and they had slings with which they could hurtle rocks. The leader directed his hunters to slowly force the Chua to move toward the edge of the canyon. They could do this by continuing the encirclement and jabbing at the monster to keep it moving without the monster being able to grab a hunter because of the distraction. All the time, the hunters kept moving toward the canyon edge.

As they approached the chasm, the hunters were directed to use their slings and aim at the monster's eyes in hopes of blinding him. At the same time, the hunters kept moving Chua toward the ravine's lip. As the great monster got close to the gorge, the hunters came from around his back side leaving nothing but space between Chua and eternity. Slowly it moved backwards, the hunters pelting his eyes with rocks, the monster clawing at his face, and slowly, slowly edging toward its eminent death.

Then it happened. That last step found no ground under his foot—there was nothing but air. It toppled over the cliff, and with a screaming roar, disappeared into the void, the sound slowly fading over a period of about 30 seconds until the final soft crash of its immense body on the rocks below.

The tribe held a huge celebration and feasted on the body of the dead enemy, Chua, drying the remainder for the months of future needs. It was claimed that the horns were saved, but nothing of that sort exists, so the old man telling the tale said that it was just a myth with nothing to back it up.

However, less than 200 miles away in the Petrified Forest, dinosaur fossil remains have been found.

Luckless Larry

By Chuck Northup

Larry was not always luckless. He once had a job that paid enough to keep him in an apartment with food to eat. He didn't own a car—they were too expensive—so he used his feet, or the bus, to get around.

Larry was a disk jockey for a small broadcasting radio station in Los Angeles. As most people may know, with the coming of the digital age, the radio business is slowly going away with the advent of podcast and streaming, so those stations that played music are not being listened to much anymore. As a result, advertisers are disappearing, and stations are going bankrupt.

Larry was earning less than $35,000 per year that didn't allow much room for luxuries or even modest living. Fortunately, he was not married, so there was no family to worry about housing or feeding. He had only his own life to keep up.

He was unable to save any money for emergencies, so when his job vanished, he couldn't pay the rent for his apartment, so he shacked up with a friend for a few months. That friend couldn't keep paying for Larry's upkeep very long, so Larry landed on the street.

He had no qualifications for any specific job. He had the gift of gab that carried him through the disc jockey work, but there were no other jobs that needed a loquacious mouth. He attempted to find work as a waiter, but found none. Jobs were scarce.

As he became a homeless person, his appearance got worse, and applying for work became impossible, looking the way he did, but he soon discovered that Los Angeles had some recently installed shower accommodations at their shelters for the homeless with lockers, and he could launder his clothes there. They also had spare clothing, a barber, and counselors to help those who were seeking jobs and homes.

Larry found protection from the elements in the library. He could disappear into the stacks or sit and read all day. In the evening, just before closing, he would hide in a closet near the main entrance until the doors were locked each night at nine. Then he would come out and sleep in the staff lounge that had a couch, table, sink, and microwave where workers ate their lunches.

He carried a briefcase from his prior job to hold a few of his belongings and whatever food he would need at night, and it held a flashlight to use when the library lights were out. During the day, he would stay outdoors and enter the library late in the afternoon. To avoid being detected he would stay in distant parts of the building, changing his location daily.

One day, however, an assistant librarian of about his age came up to him as he was reading at a table. What better place to find an intelligent man than at a library? It was certainly better than a bar, and besides, she didn't drink. She was simply being friendly and said, "Hi, my name is Serena, and I work here. I've seen you come in here quite often. Are you a college student?"

Larry lied when he answered, "No, I'm a disc jockey at the KNHX radio station."

"Oh, how exciting!" He did not mention that the station was now bankrupt and had not operated for several months.

She continued, "That sounds like a wonderful job. You must be very talkative."

"They nick-named me 'Larry the Lip' around the station since I talked so much."

She admitted, "We don't talk much around here. It's nice to have a conversation with someone occasionally. I've seen you in here often, and I thought I'd like to meet you. Where do you live?"

"Downtown," Larry said evasively.

"Have you had dinner yet?" she asked.

"No, I have a sandwich in my briefcase for later."

She went on, "I work the late shift, and I'm on my dinner break. I eat in the staff lounge where they let us keep our food. I love to converse with someone when

I eat. Would you care to join me? I'll tell them you're a friend."

Larry was surprised that this pleasant young woman would ask him to have dinner with her. He was concerned that he might be discovered, but he weighed that against being close to a beautiful woman and decided to go along.

"That would be nice. Where is the lounge?" he queried already knowing all about the lounge where he slept at night.

"It's around toward the back of the building. Just follow me."

She showed him a seat at the table and got a frozen dinner out of the freezer and put it into the microwave. She went to the coffee maker, and over her shoulder she asked, "Would you like a cup of coffee?"

He answered in the positive and she brought two mugs to the table and sat down. "My dinner will be ready in a couple of minutes. I'll get a plate for you to put your sandwich on."

Larry opened his briefcase surreptitiously so she wouldn't see what he had in it. He got out a newspaper-wrapped sandwich, unwrapped it, and put it on the plate she had furnished, while hiding the newspaper. They spoke about his job and how dull it really was just playing records and waiting until they were finished to add a few remarks off his head. He told her how the station plays 24 hours, and Larry had the early wake-up shift starting at five a.m., lasting until two in the afternoon, with an hour off for eating.

She told him that it did sound kind of boring, "What sort of music do you play?

"Our station specializes in jazz."

"That's why I haven't heard you. I enjoy classic, and have a big collection of symphonies. My job starts about the time yours ends and lasts until we close at nine. It's not boring at all. I meet lots of people—most of them nice. I get asked a bunch of questions all the time, and I tell them how to find the answers. To get this job, I had to have a Master's degree in Librarianship. What sort of education did you need for your work?"

Larry was embarrassed. He said, "The job is pretty easy. The only requirement is to be able to make up fill-in chatter on cue—and of course, to be able to put the needle on records. I never even finished high school. I'm a drop-out. The station has six DJs, and none of them has a college education. That's one reason they can pay us so little."

She asked, "What kind of reading do you like?"

"I'm working my way through your collection of mysteries. There are enough here to keep me busy the rest of my life."

They continued pleasant conversation until her break was over. As Serena went back to work, she said, "If you come in tomorrow, we can have dinner together again, if you'd like."

"I would like that," Larry answered. He went back to a table to read.

Serena returned to her desk and spoke with another staff member. "I just met a wonderful man," she said excitedly. He comes in here almost every day, and I just met him and had dinner with him. He's a DJ at KNHX, the jazz station. He can sure make good conversation."

The other staff member answered with a question, "I used to listen to that station and loved it, but I'm unhappy now. They closed a couple of months ago, didn't they?"

"Really?" Serna questioned. "I'll look that up."

She did just that, and discovered the truth: KNHX laid off all its employees and closed down due to bankruptcy. Larry was out of work. 'That's why he spent all this time in the library. He probably didn't have enough to eat either. She wondered how he lived. She liked him and didn't want to embarrass him, so she kept quiet about her newly-found knowledge.

The next day, Larry showed up as usual, late in the afternoon. Serena approached him at her dinner break and said, "Hi, Larry. I see that you're back. Would you like to join me at dinner again tonight?"

"Sure. I have a sandwich again, and we can eat together."

As they walked back to the lounge, Serena said, "I couldn't stand seeing you eating only a cold sandwich, so I brought along an extra frozen dinner for you, would you like that instead?"

Larry answered jokingly, "That would likely destroy my Mediterranean diet, and I'll put on some pounds, but I would like that."

As they ate, Serena said, "the weekend is coming up, and I have enough seniority to get both days off. I haven't been to the beach for a long time, and since the weather is really good, would you like to go to the shore with me?"

"Well, I have no car, and I don't drive. We'd have a tough time getting there."

"Don't worry. I have a car, so I'll drive. Where can I pick you up?"

This brought up some problems. He had no bathing suit. He had no home. He thought fast.

"You could never find my place," he said truthfully, "so I'll meet you on a nearby corner."

He named a street corner near the city shelter. He could hopefully get a pair of swim trunks there from the cast-offs.

"That would be great! How about if I pick you up at ten on Saturday? It's only a short drive to the coast. I'll pack a lunch and throw in a blanket and beach umbrella. You just bring yourself and maybe a straw hat."

"Fine. It's a date! I'll meet you on Saturday.

The only trunks Larry could find were a size too small and were of a skimpy style, but he managed to get them on. They were so tight, they showed off his manliness embarrassingly. He was also able to find a straw hat—a little big, but OK, and a pair of dark glasses. He was ready.

The day went gloriously. Serena had fixed an enormous lunch of fried chicken, salad, a big bag of chips and even a pudding dessert. She provided soft drinks in a portable icebox, and they ate under the beach umbrella with everything spread out on a blanket. They both enjoyed the water greatly, diving into the waves and dunking each other playfully.

She had brought along some suntan oil and he opportunely complied when she asked him to spread it on her. As he reached her belly and chest, his shorts almost burst, and this did not escape her attention. When it was her turn to apply the oil on his chest and belly, he could not hide his bodily response.

They left mid-afternoon and on the way into town, she placed her hand on his on the front seat.

"Would you like to stop by my place for a while? We can have a little snack for dinner before I take you home," she asked with an inviting smile.

"Yes, I'd like to see where you live if that's not too much trouble."

As soon as the door closed behind them, they grasped each other and kissed. She took his hand and guided him into the bedroom.

As they undressed, he stated, "what a relief to get out of these tight trunks!"

Later, in the living room, she told him,

"When you're dealing with a librarian, they have immense research possibilities. I know that you are out of work. I'm aware that your station closed several months ago. Many of your fellow workers are in the same situation. Are you homeless?"

He admitted sheepishly, "Yes, I am. I lost my apartment three months ago, and I've been unable to find work."

"How do you live? "Where do you find food and shelter?"

"I operate out of the city shelter. They, as well as many churches, provide hot meals. The shelter provides us with lockers to store our goods, instead of carrying around a bag, and washers and dryers to clean our clothing. They have cast-off clothing—often new ones simply out of style—and donated by stores. There's a counsellor to help us find homes and work. I have an appointment with him tomorrow with a possible job offer.

"I hesitate to tell you, but I live at the library where you work. I hide in a closet when you close, and come out when the door is locked. I sleep in the lounge."

"Wow! That's quite a story. I don't have room in my home, or I'd let you stay here. However, the library is still open, and I can drop you off in front so you can say there tonight, but you're going to have to find another place to sleep. You'll eventually be discovered and perhaps be arrested."

"Thank you for being quiet about my mischief. I'll try the best I can."

Larry had his appointment the next day, and the counsellor told him, "A TV station is seeking a host for a new game show. Many applicants will show up, but I can give you a good recommendation for your good moral values. The interview will be in a week. We have suits to offer you for the session. Good luck."

Meanwhile, Larry continued his stay at the library. At closing time a few days later, one of the staff ladies was just stepping outside when she realized it was raining. She went back to the desk and asked if there were any spare umbrellas somewhere because it wasn't raining when she came.

Someone said that there were some left by patrons and are stored in the closet by the front entrance.

The entire building heard her scream! Others who were also leaving rushed over of the closet to find out what was wrong.

"There's a man in there!" she blurted.

The group peered into the doorway to see a head peering over a pile of boxes like a gopher sticking his head out of his burrow.

Larry was discovered.

"Come out!" a staff member ordered.

Serena saw and heard the ruckus and knew what was happening. She immediately spoke up, "That man is a friend of mine. He is seeking work and has no home. I know he's been staying here safely, but he has harmed nothing. He's a good man, down on his luck."

A janitor spoke up saying, "He can't stay here, but I have extra room at my house. He can come home with me."

Serena stepped up and said, "I'll vouch for him. His name is Larry."

"That's good enough for me," answered the janitor. "Come with me, Larry."

The job interview at the TV station went exceedingly well. The recommendation from the city counsellor made a big impression, and Larry's experience on radio was known by a couple of the interviewers. His reputation for gift of gab was well-known, and he got the job.

"Your salary will start at $42,000. You will require a new outfit each time you appear, but we have a wardrobe department that'll take care of that.

"We know you are homeless, so we'll give you an advance on your salary so you can get a place to stay. You will report to work tomorrow so we can get you signed up, but the show will not start until next month—we need the time for your training and advance publicity. See you tomorrow."

Larry went back to the library and told Serena the good news. She was overjoyed. They saw much of each other in the coming months, and they eventually ended up living together.

Marriage of Convenience
By Chuck Northup

Brian found it impossible to put on his support socks to aid his varicose veins because his paunch did not permit him to reach his feet, so he called upon his neighbor, Serena, to help him get them up to his knees, and she could do the stressful job easily.

Serena stood only 5′ 2″ and could not reach the shelves in her closets or kitchen so she called upon Brian, who towered more than six feet tall, to get things out of reach for her. It was a complimentary plan.

This arrangement normally took place rather early in the morning for Brian so he usually ended up having breakfast with Serena in her apartment. They both lived in Privara, an upscale senior complex in California that provided each of them a studio apartment of generous proportions.

They were both products of former marriages and now widowed with grown families. They found they got along together just fine and had many thoughts and pursuits in common. They both enjoyed music and attended the concerts in nearby cities. They were also both art lovers, and each had an extensive (and expensive) art collection, his in Native American ceramics and hers in Oriental silk embroideries.

Brian could no longer drive because he couldn't pass the vision test—he wore very thick lenses in dark-rimmed glasses, so heavy they had to be held on his head with a strap. Serena, however, still drove and took both of them to the many different places they enjoyed—restaurants, plays, concerts art shows, and various stores.

They both enjoyed each other's company greatly and were seen together constantly. Their families had met each other and agreed that the two made a good pair. They were still in their seventies and got about easily. It was not long before they talked about living together. Their children thought it was a good idea as well because it would take the worry off their minds of daily care if either became unable to handle daily affairs. They felt that arrangement would be similar to having a constant, live-in caregiver at no added cost.

Neither of their studio apartments was sufficient for their collections so they upgraded to a two-bedroom apartment with a large patio and larger interior to handle their art collections. Brian enjoyed dabbling in the garden and this allowed him to do more planting than his former studio permitted. Serena also enjoyed flower arranging and, with Brian's gardening, supplied her cut flowers to put into the apartment.

Then an interesting event occurred. They decided to get married, and no one could say why. This required some family planning. They called their families together, some by Zoom because of distance, and spoke of their plans and what they wanted to achieve. After much discussion, a solution was reached. A lawyer was engaged and the entire plan was put down on paper.

Brian and Serena agreed this was not a marriage for love—it was for convenience. Each decided they would keep his or her assets separate, but they would live on the income from their investments in a joint marriage. Their incomes appeared nearly equal anyway and this arrangement would not cause any disagreement. They also made a will that left their children without any great inheritance, but their collections and assets would be donated to charities. Their children were all engaged in prosperous endeavors and needed no further wealth.

Several years passed and many grandchildren were presented to both families. Many times, a reunion was held in a local hotel, where everyone got to meet everyone else. Brian and Serena were a happy couple who admired their combined family.

One day they flew to Europe on a trip to a major museum opening. They purchased a few inexpensive pieces that were on sale from the museum's surplus, but then, a terrible accident happened. The flight for their return trip crashed into the Atlantic Ocean, and all lives were lost.

Their will was probated, and a large contribution consisting of their combined collections was made to their favorite charity. The charity distributed the ceramics and embroideries to appropriate galleries and institutions, and today their collection rests in several museums around the world.

But the probate also uncovered a great secret. Brian had no fortune. He was only a few months short of poverty. His ceramic collection was of great value, but it was purchased during more prosperous times. His arrangement and later marriage with Serena were for her money. He married her because he would be penniless soon.

The probate uncovered yet another secret. Serena also had no fortune. Her invaluable collection was also purchased in her wealthier times. She quickly agreed to the marriage because she too would be destitute soon and with that wedding, she would be able to live off his money.

Neither knew of the others paucity. Both thought the other was wealthy. They both lived off a diminishing checking account that would soon be gone. They were able to maintain their affluent life style only by writing draughts on their rapidly vanishing accounts.

The truth became apparent to both after their marriage, when they made their first joint income tax report to the government. They had no income to report. They had both been playing the same game. They kept their finances apart from the other to maintain the secret.

This disclosure was the beginning of an elaborate plot. To avoid public and family embarrassment, they would keep this ruse secret from all relations, become frugal by adhering to an austerity program, and cut way back on jaunts to favorite eateries, concerts, and galleries. To avoid spending at Christmas time, they would use their collections as gifts. When they would reach the near end of the dwindling finances, they would simply fly to some unfamiliar country on the Mediterranean and disappear.

Time and money finally did reach the tilting point. With a little research, they found the opening of a new wing of a major museum and used this reason to go to Europe. They would intentionally purchase a few inexpensive items for their collections and ship them home to give the impression that they would be returning themselves, even though they had no intention of going home. They had even purchased a return flight ticket.

Instead, after the museum opening, they flew to Egypt and then bussed to Siwa, an oasis near the Libyan border. Because Siwa is a tourist attraction, it is a bustling town of about 35,000 people, all living in beam and sandstone buildings, and has numerous hotels, so Brian and Serena chose a cheap one for their purposes.

They purchased a rope and hooked it to a sturdy beam in the room's ceiling. They both stood on a table and put the loose ends of the rope around their necks and tied them tightly. Brian then kicked the table away. Death was immediate with broken necks at the end of a two-foot drop.

Their bodies were found the next day, but since they had registered under assumed names and paid cash, and they had destroyed any identifying papers, their identities were unknown, and they were buried in what amounted to a potter's field.

Even though they never arrived at home, their inexpensive purchases did arrive on a separate flight, and those were sent to the charity which then distributed them. There were no other monies to add to the charitable gifts, and, as pre-arranged, no money was left to distribute to their families.

The coincidental downed flight became a major news story, providing an unintended reason for the couple's death, and their double shame was never known.

Yawateg
By Chuck Northup

"Marge, this computer is acting up again. Now it won't print," said Rory in a storm of frustration.

"Rory," remarked his patient wife, "You've been complaining about that computer for months. Why don't you get a new one? You've had that one for years. They've probably got much better ones now, and prices may have come down."

"I think I'll take your advice. Every time I sit down at this damned thing, something goes wrong. I'll stop by the computer store today."

Rory walked into *Computers-Are-Us* at the mall downtown. A clerk greeted him by asking, "May I help you, sir?"

The clerk was a young man who appeared to have just gotten out of grammar school, but Rory, now in his sixties, realized that electronics are the meat and vegetables of young peoples' diet today. Only a few days ago Rory asked his 10-year-old grandson about getting Rory's iPhone to change the color of the screen, and his grandson achieved it with a few flicks of his fingers.

The young sales clerk took one look at this old man coming into the store and thought, "I'll have a tough job selling this grayhead anything. He probably wants the cheapest thing in the shop."

Rory said, "My computer had worn out. I've had it almost ten years, and I suppose there are many improvements I could use. Why don't you show me your finest equipment for home use?"

The clerk was amazed, and answered, "Certainly, sir. I can show you the latest laptops that we've received," and he took Rory to a special exhibit in the store.

"This computer will do nearly anything you desire. It has the most recent AI, that's artificial intelligence, that electronic engineers have been able to come up with. We received this only yesterday, so I have not become thoroughly familiar with all of its features, but the operation manual that comes with it will explain every detail."

Rory spotted the price tag and said to the clerk, "That price is much lower than I expected. If I keep this on for another ten years, it'll cost me only a few dollars each month."

The clerk offered, "We will let you try it out for 30 days at no extra charge."

Rory told him, "Wrap it up. I'll take it. It'll be good to get a computer that really works."

Rory set up the new computer on his desk and began to read the owner's manual. That book was huge—438 pages, and Rory soon grew tired of reading it. He set it aside and decided to just start fiddling around. He had noticed that there were about ten pages of special keyboard actions that did unusual things.

The simplest ones were single key strokes such as moving to the end of a sentence or moving up to the previous paragraph. There were two-key, three-key and four-key strokes as well that did far more complicated moves. It would take several weeks to learn a lot of them to the point that he could use them easily.

But the latest innovation was the five-key stroke. The most complex moves were the five-keystrokes that took very careful maneuvering with his fingers to reach all five keys at the same time. These key moves came with a special cautioning that said WARNING: These are very advanced moves. Before using them, read your owner's manual very carefully."

Rory turned to the section in the manual that covered special moves. He found that one move labeled EDITOR permitted him to edit and rewrite a composition. As an author, Rory wasn't too sure he wanted a machine to do his editing so he ignored this one. Another special function called TRANSLATOR was to change all the writing into another language which was one he would never use. There were several more items on the list that were of doubtful use, but the one titled YAWATEG had him puzzled.

Under this heading it said, 'This special function was designed for those who needed fresh thoughts or a change of attitude. It will take as much time as desired, so be certain that enough time is allowed. **IMPORTANT:** <u>you must place your wireless mouse in your pocket before operating this function</u>. The mouse will permit you to reverse the function by pressing the right button twice quickly.

The manual continued. Before depressing the keys, type a short, seven words or less, description of a place you would like to be. Then place your fingers on <u>CTRL</u>, <u>Tab</u>, <u>Back Slash</u>, <u>p</u>, and <u>Comma</u> **all at once.**

Rory had only a few more minutes before dinner so he thought he would wait to do this for another time, but he figured this delay would give him time to think of a good place. It was deep in winter at the time, and he thought it might be nice to be in a warmer place. He would give this some thought overnight.

In the morning, Rory went outside to pick up the newspaper and was greeted by a load of snow dropping off the porch roof onto his head just as he walked under it. This little event convinced him that he would like to be in a warm place. At breakfast, he told Marge all about his new computer purchase and that it had the latest advancements—many that he had never heard of before. He told her he was going to try them out this morning, so if he doesn't come out of his den for a while, don't be concerned.

He took his cup of coffee into the den and closed the door. He got out the owner's manual and turned to the page about special functions. Since he had been considering writing an article about Kenya, he typed the words 'country of Kenya,' put the wireless mouse into his shirt pocket and pressed the five-key indicated under the title YAWATEG.

Instantly, he was transported to Kenya. He looked about and saw miles of level, dry land with flat-topped trees, parched grass, and piles of animal dung. There were no people. It was like being in a magazine photo of the country, but he could move around and even touch things and smell the air. It was hot. He realized he was near the equator because he was starting to sweat. He thought this was a little hotter than he desired and not really, a comfortable place to be. He dug into his shirt pocket and retrieved the wireless mouse, clicked twice on the right button, and was immediately returned to his seat in front of his computer. He reached for his coffee and found it to be cold. This made him look at his watch to see how long he had been gone. That figured out to be about 20 minutes.

That was a learning experience. He must be careful and thoughtful about what he types. He wanted to try again so he thought a while and finally typed Hawaii into his computer and put the mouse into his pocket and typed the five characters.

Voila! There he was in what appeared to be a beautiful tropical island. There were no buildings or people. There was only a sandy beach and forest alongside the ocean. Rory thought there would-be hula dancing girls in grass skirts or perhaps some men with hand drums—maybe a couple of night clubs, hotels and restaurants. Instead, he saw only beautiful beach and ocean complete with a comfortable temperate climate, so he strolled along the beach for a while, threw a few stones into the ocean, and even found an empty shell along the shore. This was wonderful—but lonely. Rory guessed that artificial intelligence could not dream up people or other live things like nuisance bugs that all looked alike—only places that appeared to be taken by a professional photographer with perfect lighting and no one in the photo. But these places were awfully good if he chose well. He stretched out on the sand and sun-bathed and even dozed off for a few minutes. When he awakened, he found that he had gotten sunburned. How was he going to explain this to Marge?

He also realized that there was no food. He was hungry so he went into the forest to see if he could find anything to eat. There were coconuts, and he managed to open one with a lot of work using a sharp rock. That nut satisfied him for the time, but he wondered how he would get some *real* food at any other time or place. He thought he had been there long enough so he double-clicked and returned home.

This time, he found he had been gone over four hours. His wife was worried about him not coming out of his den for so long, but she didn't disturb him — Jake always hated to be disturbed. When he did come out, his wife immediately saw his sunburned face and asked him about it. Rory made up a quick excuse about some new shaving lotion that irritated his skin. He also decided in his mind that he would lock his door hereafter.

It was about two weeks later that Rory took another trip with his computer. He was gone over six hours exploring a Civil War battleground that he had been writing about and wanted to obtain some first-hand experience. During his absence, Marge became very concerned and knocked on his door. He heard the knocking in his ear while strolling around the battlefield at **Antietam,** double-clicked, and returned home to answer his wife.

Marge said, "you were so quiet locked up in your room that I was worried something might have happened to you. Did you get a lot of writing done?"

Rory had done no typing at all, but he told her, "I was busy studying, but I'll leave the door unlocked as long as no one barges in."

Marge asserted, "I always knock, but if I have a visitor, I'll tell them to stay out."

What Rory found out was that while his mind was away in some distant place, his body was still in his chair seated in front of his computer. The interesting thing, however, was that whatever happened to his body on his travel, actually happened to his body at home, such as the sunburn. His 'at-home' body went into a coma-like state and appeared that he was sleeping.

The feature on his new computer helped in his writing. Rory's main source of income was articles in magazines, and this new method of research allowed him to write from actual examples and true experiences to add greater value to his writing, thereby increasing his sales.

This YAWATEG feature had its drawbacks. The most serious was the mouse, or more importantly, forgetting the mouse on his journeys. He had no idea what would happen if he forgot his mouse. What would happen to his travelling body? Would his home-body simply die? Would Marge take his coma-like body to a hospital and attempt to revive it? Rory decided to buy an extra mouse to keep with him, just in case.

That happened in a couple of months when he took a trip to research some of the islands of the Carribean, and forgot to take his mouse with him.

After spending about two hours—he had purposely shortened his trips to avoid worrying Marge—he discovered he had forgotten his mouse. He went into panic mode until he remembered the spare that he kept with himself at all times. He double-clicked and, sure enough, it worked! He was back home safely.

Rory's writing had taken a huge step and his income with it. He was being accepted regularly in magazines because of his well-researched writing. He had even started a book that showed promise. Marge never knew about these sojourns that he took, but Rory always made sure of two things: take the mouse and eat a full meal before going.

Kotobuki

By Chuck Northup

The scroll was gorgeous! Mark asked the salesperson what the writing meant. The Japanese store clerk said "kotobuki."

"That's a nice word, but what does it mean in English?" Mark continued.

The clerk was very fluent in English, perhaps other languages as well, so he was able to discuss the sale with intelligence. He told Mark, "The word has several meanings—all good. That's why it is used so much. It means long life, celebration, rejoicing, and happy event. It is also the surname of many people, even the name of a railway station."

The seller saw he had an interested customer—perhaps he could entice him to purchase this nice scroll wall hanging. He decided to pull out all of the stops.

"This scroll has far more importance than the promising phrase emblazoned on it. It was done by a Living National Treasure, Moboru Fujinami."

The clerk knew this was a lie, but what did a stupid tourist know, anyway? Mark became more interested. He asked, "What is a Living National Treasure?"

The clerk answered, "It is the greatest honor that can be bestowed on a person. There are several categories among the crafts, and brush calligraphy is one of them. This particular artist is no longer living, so his works have become more valuable and will continue to increase in value as time goes by."

Mark inquired, "What is the price of this scroll?" The deceitful clerk saw an opportunity to make a bonus on this sale, so he quoted a price twice what the store charges, feeling he could pocket the difference.

Mark was surprised by the amount, and with bargaining in mind, he proposed, "That's quite expensive—could you shave a little off the price?"

The clerk squinted his eyes and pursed his lips as he put his hand up to his mouth in an expression of heavy thought. "I am unable to reduce the price, but I could cheat the government a little by not charging you any sales tax."

Mark knew the tax was 10% so he thought that would be a good discount.

"Fine, I'll buy it. Wrap it carefully so I can carry it back in hand to the U.S. Oh, and would you write the artist's name on a slip of paper, and put it into the package, please."

Mark was not interested in keeping the scroll for himself. It would not fit into the décor of his home. But, he was thinking of his close friend, Phil, who was a Japanophile. Phil's home was filled with beautiful

Japanese objects, and Mark felt he could get back his money from Phil by selling the scroll to him. If Phil didn't want it, he would simply sell it online. It had plenty of inherent value so he felt he could dispose of it easily. It would be like selling a Monet or other famous artist's work. Collectors would probably bid up the price. He would not take advantage of his friend, however. He would sell it to him at the price he had paid.

The clerk showed him something extra. The scroll came in the box. It was a piece of beauty all by itself, and Mark began to glow even more as the clerk carefully wrapped the purchase.

The trip was over. Mark reached home with his treasure—the only thing of real value that he had purchased in Japan. The rest of his baggage was trinkets he found that he could give his kids or friends.

The next day Mark went to Phil's house with his prize. After some small talk and a drink that Phil had proffered, Mark brought out—with some fanfare—the box with the scroll to show Phil. He told Phil the story the clerk had told him and all about it being the work of a Living National Treasure. Phil knew all about that designation and had a few items of that nature in his own collection.

Mark said, "I can't use this in my house. I bought it thinking you would like it for your own. It's so expensive I can't just give it to you, but I'll sell it to you for the price I paid. If you don't want it, I'll sell it online to someone else."

"No, Mark. You won't sell it to someone else. I'll buy it at your price and feel lucky that I didn't have to pay an importer his fee. You have seen my collection so much that you seem to know what I like. Your taste is good, and you chose something very nice." Then he added, "You know now that I've increased my collection, so I'll have to increase my insurance!"

In fact, the next day Phil called his insurance agent to increase his coverage, and the agent told him it had been some time since he did so and he should have his collection re-assessed. He told Phil that he would send an assessor by in a day or two.

The assessor showed up on time and went carefully through all of Phil's collection of Japanese treasures and antiquities of which he had many. He handed the list to Phil who checked out the latest findings.

Phil came upon the price shown for the scroll he had just purchased from Mark and found it was priced at about half of what he had paid Mark.

"You have assessed this scroll at such a low price. Don't you realize that this is the work of the Living National Treasure, Moboru Fujinami?""

The assessor said to Phil, "This is a beautiful scroll worth every penny I assessed, but it is a work of

Kojiwara Hashimi, a well-known calligrapher, not a National Treasure. See, here's his signature."

Phil looked, but said, "I can't read kanji, so I don't know what it says."

"That's the trouble. Tourists go to Japan and buy things not knowing what they are because they can't read any of the language. If you paid more than this, you've paid too much."

Phil glowered at the assessor and said, "I don't blame you. I purchased it blindly. I didn't check the signature as I should have."

The assessor soothed Phil quickly by saying, "Your collection has appreciated so much in value since the last time you should be happy with those new figures even though your insurance costs will go up. I wouldn't worry about a few hundred dollars that you overspent on this nice scroll. Who knows? Maybe that artist will be named a National Treasure also—he's very good. If that should happen, you will have something very valuable."

Then Phil said, "I'll keep that in mind. Thank you."

The next time Phil saw Mark, he told him about the assessor.

Mark was very shame-faced and said, "I'm really sorry. I apologize for the mistake. I should have checked before I bought. I trusted the clerk at the store. I'll give you your money back."

"No, Mark. I'd just like the difference in price. You won't be out everything."

"No, I can't impose a fake on you. You're too much of a friend to do that. I was mistaken, and you shouldn't have to suffer."

Phil remarked, "Just let it go for a while. Let's see what happens."

Nearly a year passed, and Phil was decidedly cool toward Mark and they were still uneasy friends.

Mark had another business trip to Japan, so he asked Phil if he could take the scroll with him to get his money back. Phil agreed.

Mark returned to the store and sought out the owner. He told the owner the entire story. The owner said that clerk is no longer working there. He was not honest so he was discharged. Another scroll was there—not kotobuki—but one by a real National Treasure. I'll let you have it at the price you should have been quoted—about half of what you paid, if that is OK with you."

Mark looked at the scroll and found it to be equally beautiful. He agreed with the new arrangement and took the new scroll.

When he reached home, he approached Phil with the hope that he could make amends for his error. He presented Phil with the scroll and half of his money back.

"Here, Phil. This is yours. I wish to give this to you to replace the other."

Phil literally beamed when he saw the new scroll.

"This is just perfect. I recognize the signature. It is far more valuable than the other one. Let me give you more for it."

"No, Phil. It is yours to keep with my pleasure and the hope that we can become good friends again."

Phil spread his arms, and stepping toward Mark, gave him a big hug.

April Fool

By Chuck Northup

The Salem witch trials were a series of hearings and prosecutions of people accused of witchcraft in colonial Massachusetts between February 1692 and May 1693. More than two hundred people were accused. Thirty were found guilty, and nineteen were executed by hanging. One other man, Giles Corey, was pressed to death for refusing to plead, and at least five people died in jail.

The date was March 31, 1694, just one year following the infamous Salem witch trials. Witchcraft was still fresh in the minds of the delusory residents. Spring had supposedly begun ten days previously, but the sun had begun to shine only this day. Geoffrey was enjoying the beautiful change from winter by taking a walk in a nearby park.

He found a bench in the sun and sat down to soak in a few rays. There were several others walking around in the park taking advantage of this first day of sunshine, but he noticed that many strolled with their heads down for no particular reason. They seemed to be watching the ground immediately in front of them instead of holding their heads up to see the scenery passing by. This realization motivated him to study and count the number of people with their eyes on the ground instead of looking forward.

After he reached the count of fifteen, he thought of a simple joke to play on them for the next morning, which was April fool's Day. He wanted to have a bit of fun on this lazy day. He would give them something to see as their eyes were on the ground.

He went home and sought out a jar of glue. That evening, making sure he had some coins in his pocket, Geoffrey returned to the same area, and when no one was nearby, he glued a pine tree shilling (British denominations were still being used in the Colonies) to the cobblestone walkway a short distance away from where he would sit, so he could easily observe what happened. He stood on the coin until he was certain the metal was solidly fastened to the pavement, and then he returned home to allow the glue to solidly set and become hard.

Early the next morning, he returned to his viewpoint on the bench. It was not long before someone stopped to pick up the coin, but try as he may he was unsuccessful and became slightly frustrated and angry with himself for being so stupid. The coin was so attractive that others passing by couldn't resist stopping to pick it up, and soon a small crowd had gathered to watch another man attempt to dislodge it.

Geoffrey just watched and giggled. In a short time, the group's attention was directed to Geoffrey, who was laughing and enjoying the antics of the several coin seekers.

A member of the crowd got down on his knees, bent his head low, and inspected the coin more carefully and said loudly, "It's a <u>witch</u> coin!"

He was referring to the first coin minted in America, the pine tree shilling, which was 1/20th of a pound, the currency used by the colonists. It had been struck about twenty years before the witch trials and had become associated with those proceedings. Many people carried these coins in their pockets with the supposition that they would ward off witchcraft with their jingling. Some believed that the pine tree on the coin was a symbol of witches being hanged on a tree.

That man's announcement caused the crowd to suspect the laughing Geoffrey and one shouted, "That man laughing at us must be a witch!"

Another yelled, "Just listen to him cackle—he even <u>sounds</u> like a witch!"

Geoffrey stopped laughing right away. He said to the crowd that now surrounded him, "That was just an April Fool joke—I was only being flippant," but his defenses were all in vain.

One man cried out, "We'll show ye what we do with witches—tie him up!"

The group had suddenly become an unruly mob, and the chant started up, "Hang the witch—Hang the witch—Hang the witch—"

They roughly pulled the scarf from his neck and bound his hands behind his back. Another man stripped the belt from his pants and, making a loop with the buckle, tossed the loop over his head and placed it around Geoffrey's neck, while others held him as he was struggling to escape.

They dragged him screaming and yelling—he could barely breathe—only grunts could be heard with his throat tied. They found a nearby tree with a low branch just over their heads and tossed the loose end of the belt over it, and two men pulled the belt, lifting Geoffrey off his feet a few inches, with his neck against the branch and the two men holding him aloft.

The crowd ripped off his clothing and stole his pocket watch, wallet and pocket change, leaving him naked, dangling from the tree.

Geoffrey struggled, his eyes bulging and tongue reaching out for air while his legs were engaged in the dance of death. Since they had not broken his neck with a jerk at the end of a fall, he was frantically and slowly strangling to death. His legs finally stopped jerking and his body went limp. They had successfully hanged an innocent person who they imagined was another witch. After waiting until they were certain he was dead, they let go of the belt, and Geoffrey dropped to the ground in a heap and was left lying on the grass, an unidentifiable corpse—evidence of a silly joke gone wrong.

Note: One from the mob went back that evening with a hammer and chisel and retrieved the coin. After all, he could take that shilling and buy a drink in those days.

Carribean Outing

By Chuck Northup

"Marge, I've found just the tour for us. It sounds great! Its best deals are in August—just when I get my vacation. Here, take a look at this ad," Sam said, as he handed the magazine over the table to his wife.

"Sam, this looks like a really inexpensive vacation. We would pay only a little over $1,200 in total. I guess they'll add tax, too, but it's still a bargain. I say, let's do it," said Marge.

"Wow! Marge, this is the first time you've ever agreed with me so quickly! I'll give them a call as soon as I get to the office and check my schedule."

"August 13th? That date will be just fine," Sam said to the travel agent, after he checked his data.

"I'll make the reservation for you and your wife. We leave from SFO at 5:00 a.m. The flight will take about 13 hours with three stops. We do not serve food on board so it would be wise to bring your own. "We do have drinks at extra cost. May I have your credit card number, please?"

Sam gave him the information and wrote down all the time data. He then asked, "What kind of clothing should we bring?"

"Everything is extremely casual in Jamaica. If you decide to go dancing, you will probably want to wear shoes instead of sandals, but otherwise plain sandals or go-aheads will do. Remember the weather is warm, but sudden rains occur, so bring cool clothing.

"Your group will have a guide assigned to you at all times. If there are no other questions, we'll meet you at SFO on the 13th."

"It's all arranged," Sam said excitingly to Marge when he returned home. "We'll leave on the 13th of

August. You'll have to pack food for the plane ride. It takes 13 hours."

"I can easily do that, but I'm not sure I can wait that long. I'm ready to leave right away," Marge added.

The day arrived and Sam and Marge went to SFO to catch their plane. They were directed to the loading area where smaller planes were used. There was a man standing near the gate with a sign with the name of the tour company. Sam and Marge went up to him and identified themselves. He told them they had to wait until all the group had arrived. Everyone soon did, and then they proceeded toward the gate.

The guide said, "Your plane is ready to load, so please step this way."

They went through the check-in and down a ramp to the tarmac. They were surprised that they had to enter from the ground. Usually, they went through a covered ramp directly into the plane. Sam questioned the guide about this and he was told that smaller planes do not load that way. They were taken to a plane nearby.

They saw a bi-plane with two propellers. As they entered, Sam said, "It looks like it holds only a few people with one row of seats on each side of the aisle, and it looks pretty old."

The guide said, "It holds eight. It's a DeHaviland, and it was in service from 1935, and we bought it from

Qantas a few years ago. It is a very sturdy plane and one of the best ones made.

"You will be comfortable—did you bring some food? We have three rest stops along the way in Albuquerque, Houston, and Miami.

"Please take your seats." Smaller planes than jets are required to fly at lower altitudes because they don't go as fast, but the atmosphere is rougher, and the ride is more uncomfortable.

The flight was very long and tiring. Everyone was uncomfortable and more than anxious to reach the airport in Jamaica. They were greeted by a bus driver who would take them the rest of the way. They groaned at the thought of getting on a bus and going on yet another journey to travel to their final destination. The bus jogged along a rough road several miles to a native village. Here was yet another surprise: there was no hotel; it was not on the beach; there was no landscaping or swimming pool. It was a native village.

The group of eight was introduced to their guide who would assist them throughout the time they were there. His name was Luis. He spoke English with a difficult-to-understand accent, but he showed them to their quarters.

They walked past many thatched houses built like teepees with poles and covered with sheets of bark. Each family had one. There was only one shower and privy for everyone to use. The running water apparently came from a large tank fed by a stream. They finally came to the place they would sleep.

It was a longhouse that originally was used by the village as a meeting place. It had been transformed into sleeping quarters for tourists. There was only one bedroom, a single privy room with a bowl and pitcher, and a central room in between. Since there were eight in the group, everyone must share the bedroom since there were no beds in the central room. Everyone simply stared at each other.

Then they took notice of the beds. They were only hammocks attached to the walls. Each one held only one person, so husband and wives could not sleep together, but there were eight hammocks in each room.

They dropped their baggage and were guided to the village center for dinner. This was cooked on an outdoor cooking arrangement. The village people were expecting the group to arrive and had dinner ready. It consisted of sea fish, crabs, and many vegetables that were grown by the village. There was a huge choice consisting of grapefruit-sized breadfruit, leafy-green callaloo, bananas, coconuts, corn, avocados, potatoes, squash, peppers and several other strange fruits. Dinner was delicious!

During dinner, the guests were treated to entertainment. Men would sing, groups would play drums, shake maracas, and beat sticks rhythmically. Women would dance in colorful clothes.

Soon, everyone was very tired from their long journey and headed for bed. The next day the guide announced it was beach day. He used a bus and took everyone in the group to a nearby beach that was outstandingly beautiful. The sand was like sugar, the palm trees towered behind the beach, and the warm sea pushed gentle waves upon the shore. An area in the nearby trees had been cleared and made into a picnic park with a table covered by a palm leaf roof where the group had lunch brought in by the villagers. Those who wanted to get out of the hot sun for a while were able to use this area.

Later, they were returned to the village to walk through the mini-store where hand-made articles of charms could be purchased. Their inventory included necklaces made from shells or wooden beads, colorful stone brooches and hats made from bark or palm leaves. Other various articles were available as well. The village was able to make some extra money in this way.

This was followed by another bountiful dinner, more entertainment and sleep. The following morning started casino day. The group was bussed to a casino in the nearest city where they could spend the day or shop in stores if they desired. Most took advantage of the excellent cuisine furnished by local restaurants, to eat a hearty lunch, and after another couple of hours, returned to the village for an evening similar to the previous ones.

The last day they flew home on the same plane, and Sam and Marge dropped into bed, completely exhausted from the uncomfortable flight. Sam admitted to Marge, "I believe that the next time we take a tour, we'll spend more money to get more amenities. I'd rather use a jet and stay in a hotel. That cheap tour we took was very nice if you don't mind playing the part of a native. We probably saw more of the real Carribean than most tourists, but I'd prefer running water and a flush toilet, and I'd rather not share a bedroom with anyone except you in the same bed—not be alone in a hammock."

Betty Stearns Stories

Egypt-Here we come

By Betty Stearns

I could see excitement in Wally's eyes—and a smile. We had just finished hearing a guest speaker from Egypt at the La Canada Presbyterian Church. He was looking to fill staff openings at his school in Alexandria. He needed a school chaplain who would also serve as a minister to a community Christian church.

Just a day before, we heard Wally was out of his job as assistant pastor. The new Senior Pastor was bringing his own assistant and music director. Wally and I spoke quietly to each other. Wally remarked, "I'm thinking this passes the test: A position I would really like and a move so good and interesting for the kids."

Within minutes, we decided to inquire further. "Are we too old? We are both 40 and have 4 children."

No, the age was fine. The speaker, George Meloy, the headmaster of an American school in Alexandria, asked me, "Are you scared at the sight of blood?" "No" I answered. "Then you will be the school nurse!"

The next day George called us and we continued to explore the possibility. We were interrupted by a loud call for help from one of the kids. A heavy metal bar had landed on David's head. We explained to George that this was not a problem. Later he told us he decided that our relaxed, casual attitude would fit right in with his school.

We immediately began shopping and gathering necessities for a three-year stint in Egypt. Our kids would be growing through several sets of clothes. As we started, our youngest was 4 years old and our oldest was 11. We had a lot of work to do. We would leave in just a few weeks. It was 1965.

Our travels started with some training in New Jersey. Mary had problems with her ears on the flight from California and we were medically advised to avoid further flights as we headed overseas. We then switched plans to go by ship. The Presbyterian Board of Foreign Missions set us up in the old Henry Hudson Hotel in New York City on the fifth floor.

Very soon, we became acquainted with a man who walked his tall greyhound back and forth on our hall. On the 2nd day, he invited us to the movies where he said his brother worked and would get us in free. Without much thought, we accepted, leaving our young children in the apartment alone.

We noticed as we boarded the city bus, that our new friend kept his eyes closed, pretending to be blind, and using his pet as a service dog. After 15 minutes into the movie and hearing the dog howl who was waiting in the basement, he whispered he would need to take the dog home, but insisted we stay to enjoy the rest of the movie. He then left.

Within minutes, we woke up to the fact that we did not even know this man who now was returning to the hotel where our kids were. Breathlessly we rushed back in our panic, again on public transit. To our surprise relief, we encountered this man in the elevator and we soon found our kids were safe!

We boarded the Queen Fredericka ocean liner out of New York to cross the Atlantic. The safety drill on the ship consisted of passengers seated in the large lounge, curtains drawn. Dorothy, our 9 year old, wondered why the curtains were closed. We realized later that they served to block out the view of the lifeboats that were rusted in place, clearly not ready for any emergency.

Passing the Rock of Gibraltar was a thrill, as I had learned so much about it in my studies of world history. However the Mediterranean Sea is well known for its rough waters, and seasickness overwhelmed some of us. We stopped at Naples, Italy and stayed the night. We visited Pompeii, an ancient city devastated by the historic eruption from Mt. Vesuvius. Then on to Egypt!

As we approached Alexandria, seated on the delta of the historic Nile, I felt amazed, almost overwhelmed, to see the real thing! Housein, the school's driver, greeted us amiably while keeping the port authorities happy with a little baksish (bribe money). A short drive would deliver us to the front gate of the school.

Schutz American School was in the middle of the Schutz district after which it was named. We entered our neighborhood, where we would live for the next three years: the local tram stop; humble houses; little shops; and bakeries for pita bread. We could see clumps of olives drying on the side of dirt roads and little children in school uniforms happily making their way home.

Entering the school's front gate, with the gatekeeper waving us in, we started our life as a family living overseas. The campus was a playground for the students. Tall trees lined the perimeter wall, each tree with a treehouse. There were two wires connecting the the tree houses, one to walk on and one to hold onto over your head. My Art classes spanned K through 12. I enjoyed the uniqueness of each age group. One of my favorite projects was using ancient tiles from President Nasser's bathroom (acquired by an Egyptian doctor's wife) to make gorgeous mosaics with the students. We settled into our lives as teacher, nurse, minister, chaplain, and student. We had expected to be here for three years but this was not meant to be.

Our days in Alexandria would end unexpectedly with the "Six-Day War" between Egypt and Israel. We left for Cyprus, knowing we might not return. From there we were evacuated. Kids returned to school in the US and unrest in the Middle East continued. Our family became once again established in work, school, church and community life as the time went by.... never to return. However, what an experience it was. Celebrating Christmas on the Red Sea, riding camels around the Giza Pyramids, basking on the beaches near town, exploring the Catacombs in Alexandria, sitting in Cleopatra's Bath...and simply enjoying life along the Mediterranean coast.

A time we will never forget!

My Cyprus Story

By Betty Stearns

To help the reader better understand this true story, please consider the following:

Scene: *Schutz American School in Alexandria, Egypt – 1967.*
George: *Headmaster at Schutz American School, Alexandria, Egypt.*
Mary Lou: *Headmaster's Wife.*
Wally Stearns: *Husband and Father.*
Betty Stearns: *Wife and Mother.*
Mary: *Betty Stearns' Sister.*
John (11), Dorothy (9), David (6), Mary (5): *Stearns' Children.*

There was a knock at our apartment door. It was the headmaster, George, looking unusually serious.

"I'm not joking," he said. "Both the U.S. and the Egyptian government are saying that war is imminent, so we must be evacuated. Your family has the youngest children, so you are to be evacuated first. You need to be ready tomorrow! Pack in such a way knowing that you may never come back!"

"Oh my word is this possible? Does it have to be?" I guess I will be doing all the packing for four children while Wally checks with church officials on the Corniche.

Feeling frantic, I rushed by the pool on my way to the school office, while Mary Lou, lounging in the sun, called out, "The busier you are, the more you should relax." I kept going, with my head full of things I needed to do, but as I stopped for a moment, I felt a pit in my stomach. I began thinking of the things and people that I would have to leave behind. I thought about the rocks on our little porch that I had picked up along the coast of Cyprus; places where Paul, the apostle, likely walked. I thought of our little car, a Rover, with its automatic red arrows, which came out of the windows to announce which way we would turn. I smiled when I thought of our little Christmas tree, which was really a broomstick—(you could not get Christmas trees in Egypt.) I also thought about our friends that we might never see again.

Miraculously, we were ready to set sail for Cyprus the next day. We would go "by deck" which meant that we did not have a stateroom—we would sleep instead by spreading our own bedding on the deck. The kids were so excited. There were many others sleeping on the deck, as well. Wally entertained us all by demonstrating his "weaving" of a big hammock. He proclaimed loudly, "You'll find that the deck is hard, but I will be swinging in my hammock!" To his surprise, when he lay back in the hammock, the end ropes broke and he crashed onto the hard, wooden deck to the delight of the raucous crowd. There was a lot of clapping and laughing!

Our destination in Cyprus was Rocky Point Camp in the little village of Trodus, about 5,000 feet altitude. Huge army tents had been set up a week before. Our tent was big enough for the six of us. As we entered the tent, we saw on our left a couple of old wooden tables, two stovetop burners, a tiny oven (14x14 inches), a few crates upholding shelves, and a Betty Crocker Cake mix. This was our kitchen. The children at once checked out the positions of the cots and which one each wanted. They were obviously enjoying it—much like camping.

"Are these American army cots?" David asked. They were always excited if something was from America. "Were the cots used by American soldiers?"

As we were getting used to our new way of life, a package of Wrigley's chewing gum from America arrived. We did not know who sent it, but only knew that it came from America. It had four pieces in the package. Mary, being interested in numbers, said, "Just right for four kids!" Of course, they wanted to start chewing at once, but I put the package on the little kitchen shelf. "Let's keep it for a special occasion!" I could see disappointment and knew I would need to announce a special occasion very soon.

That evening I announced, "This is the special occasion! It is special because you each will get a stick of American Wrigley's chewing gum! I turned around to pick up the gum from the shelf, but the little package was gone! Then began several days of questioning, mostly asking David, where did you put it?

"David please tell us! David, it's understandable—so just tell us." He continued to deny it.

We finally stopped the questioning, because other more exciting things were happening. Two fathers in the camp ran over to our tent because they saw a scorpion nearby. We had all heard that if a scorpion stung you from your neck on up, you could die. The two fathers joined Wally in turning over and looking into every item in the tent—into dishes, shoes, blankets, washcloths, socks, etc. John, being the responsible older brother, held Dorothy, David, and Mary back. Then one of the men called out loudly "Hey! Look! "It's not the scorpion! It's a package of chewing gum, just under the little pink pillow."

"I cannot believe it," I thought. "I've been accusing David, and all of the time Mary has been hiding the gum under her pillow." Just then, Mary, looking pink in the face, ran out of the tent crying, tears pouring down. Within five minutes, all were happily chewing and making little airplanes out of the wrappings.

I was truly empathetic when my daughter Mary ran out of the tent. I had a similar experience in Cyprus within days. I have always been amazed and in awe of my sister Mary's ability to entertain college faculty so easily—something I always admired in her.

Ever since I saw the Betty Crocker Cake mix, I had decided that I could do as my sister did. Without thinking, I invited anyone in the camp with a birthday to come to a birthday party. I had put the cake in the oven so that it would be done just as people gathered. I had such a wonderful confident feeling of serving so many at one time, like my sister Mary!

I looked at my watch. It would be done at the right time, when the families all arrived. "The birthday cake is done." I announced to those gathered around the little oven. "Happy Birthday to all who have birthdays." Then it happened! As I opened the door of the oven, out came the cake in the shape of a moving python and it kept coming out on the table and kept coming. My face felt hot. I was hysterically laughing and crying at the same time. All I could do was run out of the tent.

If only I had read the directions for high altitude baking that was on the cake mix box. The last words I heard were, George, kindly saying – "I see a ladle here and I can soup it up for everybody."

Within a few days, the Egyptian government notified us that we could not return to Egypt, so an American adventure awaited us. We arrive in America soon thereafter. The children were focused on getting back to school.

On the first day of school, Dad's teacher said, "I too was on a vacation far away. I was in Rome and when I arrived in America, I wanted to kiss the green earth.

David raised his hand and said, "I like Cyprus better."

Maya Torngren Stories

The Man with the Trumpet

By Maya Torngren

When my husband Toby was ten years old, his family had a dog that had puppies. Since the puppies were pedigreed dogs, his father tried to sell them.

He advertised in the paper, and one would-be buyer wanted to trade a trumpet for one of the puppies. This was in the late thirties. People had little money and a lot of bartering was going on at that time. His father accepted the trumpet and told Toby that he had to learn how to play it.

Once a week, Toby took the bus from Godwin Heights, a suburb of Grand Rapids, and had his lesson at Hager Music in Grand Rapids, Michigan. As soon as he could play the trumpet, he joined the Godwin Heights school band. A few years later, he earned first chair in the band. As a reward, his father took him to the York Band Instrument Factory and bought him a brand new trumpet. He played with the band all the way through high school.

In 1946, when he was 17 years old, he joined the Army. After basic training, he was sent to Germany and there he was first a radio operator and then an armed car driver. Then one day they approached him and told him that they needed him to play in the band. He performed with the Army Band for lots of occasions, all over Germany, and even in France.

I met Toby in 1950. We fell in love and got engaged on New Year's Eve that same year. At that time, it was difficult to get permission for German girls to get married to American soldiers. We couldn't apply until three months before Toby's departure from Germany. However, Toby had to leave Germany with only a few days of notice. He was put on the so-called "pipe line," which meant a troop transport from Germany to Korea. The war was still going on at that time in Korea. Everyone was told that NOBODY gets off the pipeline—except the man with the trumpet.

When they arrived in Fort Dix, New Jersey, an MP took only Toby off the ship. Toby didn't know what was happening. They finally told him that he was being transferred to Camp Gordon, Georgia, where the band needed a trumpet player with band instrument repair experience. This, of course, was great news for both of us. Toby was with the band until he left the Army in 1953.

We finally got married on March 8th in 1952 after eleven months of red tape. We moved to the United States later that year and with four kids to support and a house to build, Toby didn't play the trumpet again for 40 years.

However, in 1993, we were visiting the small town of Winters, California (near Vacaville, where we lived for many years) and we happened upon the Yolo County Concert Band that was playing in the park. I convinced Toby to talk to the bandleader and he ended up going to the next band rehearsal. He was in several bands over the years—the *It's About Time Swing band*, the *Sonoma Hometown Band*, the *El Dorado Brass Band*, the *Oakdale Band*, and the *Mo Band*, among others. He loved playing in the band and meeting fellow musicians. It just goes to show you that it's never too late to return to a hobby you loved when you were younger.

About UP and DOWN

By Maya Torngren

The little two-letter word UP is so amazing. Although the real definition means high or higher, it is used in so many different ways. I was thinking about it the other day and came UP with the following:

"UP stairs, living it UP, giving UP, getting UP in the morning, stand UP comedy, stand UP for yourself, UP right, UP tight, and cleaning UP."

Then I asked my husband, Toby, if he could come UP with more examples of UPs. He told me, "Didn't you see that message on the Internet with the endless meanings of UP." Well, I didn't see it and was quite surprised by it. He found it for me and here it goes:

"We wake UP in the morning, at a meeting a topic comes UP, speak UP, we call UP our friends, brighten UP a room, polish UP the silver, warm UP the leftovers, clean UP the kitchen, we lock UP the house, we fix UP the old car. People can stir UP trouble, line UP for tickets, work UP an appetite, and think UP excuses. Being dressed UP is special. We open UP a store in the morning, but we close it UP at night. We seem to be pretty mixed UP about UP. When it threatens to rain, we say it is clouding UP. When the sun comes out, we say it is clearing UP. When it rains, it soaks UP the earth, when it doesn't rain for a while things dry UP. I looked UP in the dictionary and found more UPS, but I think I am not UP for any more UPS for today."

"Thank you, anonymous UP writer. You saved me a lot of work, looking UP the dictionary."

Now we come to MY reason for the interest in the word UP. When we were traveling in Europe with our four children, aged 6, 9, 12 and 13, in the 60s, we were staying in my mother's apartment. German apartments had no closets at that time. You stored your clothing in a shrank (armoire).

My sister Gerda's mother-in-law offered us a big shrank, but we had to pick it UP at her apartment. She lived on the second floor. My brother-in-law, Sepp, and his brother-in-law, Hans, offered to help Toby carry the shrank downstairs. Before I continue, I want to explain that this little English word UP and the German word AB is pronounced exactly the same; however, AB means the opposite, namely "down." As they carried the shrank downstairs, Sepp and Hans kept shouting "AB! AB"! to Toby and he kept lifting it UP... higher and higher. Luckily, I came along and told Toby that AB in German means down. Then they finally managed to carry the Shrank down with no more trouble.

Potluck

By Maya Torngren

When I first came to this country from Augsburg, Germany in 1952, one of the things that really impressed me was Potluck dinners. I had never seen so much food in one place before. I was remembering that not too long ago, living in Germany, during and shortly after the war, there were times when an extra piece of bread was a treat. Seeing all that food, it just overwhelmed me. I watched what everybody was doing and it seemed they were taking a small amount of everything on the table. I soon started to do the same thing myself.

There was lasagna, spaghetti, all kinds of potatoes, and many sorts of salads and on top of it all, desserts of all kinds, and everything went on one plate. There was only one problem for me. I couldn't bring myself to put lasagna next to pie or bean salad next to Jell-O.

What to do? Before I went through the line I picked up two paper plates, and placed the second plate under the first. After filling up my plate with all the salads and entrees, I did not pick up any desserts. After I was done with dinner, I used my second plate for dessert. I did sometimes lose out on some special desserts that had disappeared already, but having dessert separate was worth it for me. The Potluck introduced me to American cooking, all in one fell swoop, and I loved it.

There are some other varieties of potlucks. For instance, I was a member of the Oakdale garden club and once a year, we hosted a salad bar luncheon as a fundraiser for scholarships. Every member makes two huge salads. I never knew that so many salads existed. This is a very popular event. The club has been doing this for many, many years.

I still enjoy Potluck any time it is available to me. I have noticed lately that there are sometimes small paper plates available for dessert. Now I can even separate the salads from the dinner items, if I only had more hands.

Hot Dogs and Hamburgers

By Maya Torngren

Since it was Memorial Day, I wanted to make a real American dinner, and what is more American than hot dogs and potato salad?

As I was serving, I placed the bun and the hot dog on the plate. We were now ready to add all the condiments. Since I wanted to add a little German flavor, I also had some sauerkraut to add. I looked over to my husband Toby; his hot dog bun was stacked high. He neatly folded it and started eating. He ate the whole hot dog without even a crumb falling down. I, however, had trouble already with the first bite. The hot dog slid out of the bun and everything with it. I tried to stuff it back again, but that didn't work. Where I had added the sauerkraut, the whole bun was disintegrating. Toby wouldn't have even needed one napkin, while I was on my third one. I finally gave up and just ate the pieces separately.

I remember one time when my brother in-law was visiting from Germany. When he was served a hamburger, he neatly took apart the two halves and started to eat them with his knife and fork. I don't quite go to that extreme, though I probably would have had better luck. Instead, I just avoid going to special hamburger restaurants where the hamburgers are almost 3 inches high. I can just see myself fighting with that thing. My friends wanted to take me to the Fuddrucker restaurant in Manteca (they are famous for their hamburgers), but I wouldn't go. I don't want to embarrass them and I am sure I would have done so.

After a lot of thought, I came to a conclusion: to be able to eat hamburgers, hot dogs and even large sandwiches the American way, you have to be born here. We foreign-born people can't really compete.

A Very Good Place

By Maya Torngren

One of the things that comes with advancing age is that you start to forget some things. No, I am not talking about dementia or Alzheimer's disease. I'm talking about day-to-day forgetfulness. It seems like my husband and I were constantly looking for things that we had misplaced and couldn't find.

Eventually, we found most of them; sometimes the item was right in front of us. But sometimes, it was just gone.

The very worst thing you can do is to store something in a "very good place."

You can almost depend on not finding it when you need it. I remember one time I had bought Christmas presents during the year and stored them away again in a "very good place." When Christmas came along, I could not find them anywhere. I had to get new Christmas presents for my family. I think that year they received money. I finally did find everything, but much, much later.

It usually happens when you are looking for something else. I am not the only one who puts away things in a "very good place." All my friends are experiencing the same thing.

Here is the story of one of my good friends. She and her husband were going on vacation. Since there were a lot of break-ins in the area at that time, they decided to hide my friend's jewelry. Of course they found a "really good place" to hide it. Nobody would ever find it. They made sure that both saw where they put it, just in case one of them forgot. When they came back, neither one could remember the hiding place. They searched and searched, but could not find it. Time passed, and every once in a while they would search again. Then after 10 years, as they were going to move to an other home, they found it.

The other day my daughter said to me, "It seems like I am always looking for something I've lost these days. Sometimes, I never find it or find it in weird places." That made me really feel great; after all, she is 24 years younger than I.

Me and My Cane

By Maya Torngren

A couple of years ago, I suddenly lost most of my hearing in my right ear. With it, I lost some of my balance while walking, and I had to start using a cane. I really didn't like that cane, but I knew it was a necessity.

Whenever I left the house, my subconscious mind told me, "You don't really want to take that cane," and I would go out the door and lock it.

Then my conscious mind took over and told me, "Of course, you need that cane," so I went in and got it. This continued whenever I went shopping. I kept leaving my cane behind in different aisles. People would usually find me and bring it back to me. When I was at a Russian Deli in San Jose, where they have great German bread and sausages, I was at the checkout counter, when a young man came up to me trying to tell me something. Since he didn't speak English, I had a hard time finding out what he meant. He finally showed me my cane; then I knew I had left it at the bread aisle.

When you see people using canes, you know they need them to assist in their walking. However, there are exceptions: for instance, when you watch that gentleman who is the host of the ancestry program at

PBS walking with his cane, he looks so debonair. It seems like his cane is a fashion accessory.

Little did I know that a few years later, I would fall and break my hip and would need to use a walker from then on. Now, I would love to be able to walk with my cane again. Hope springs eternal!

The Christmas Cake Fiasco

By Maya Torngren

It was Christmas 1945. The war was over, but things were very bad for Germans at that time. Papa had already declared that he wouldn't celebrate Christmas this year: there was no food and there were no presents. However, Mama insisted that we would celebrate. After all, the war was over and we were all together again. She was getting a small Christmas tree and she had a surprise for us: she had saved the ingredients for her special "Philips Kuchen" for a whole year and we were finally going to have a real cake!

On Christmas Eve afternoon, while Mama was busy getting the apartment ready for Christmas, I was to make the cake. I was perfectly able to do this. I had made that cake many times in the past. Philips Kuchen was like a pound cake, but instead of baking it in loaf pans, it was baked in a large round pan. When the cake came out of the oven, I was shocked to see that it hadn't risen at all. It just sat there, flat as a pancake and hard as a rock. At first I couldn't understand what happened. But when I called Mama, she looked at the cake, then at me and shouted, "How could you use the whole wheat flour instead of the white flour?" She had made some baked goods with the whole wheat flower and potatoes (yes, potatoes) earlier in the day. My cake was edible, but not very tasty. Of course, I couldn't bake the cake over again. There was no more butter, no more sugar, and there were no more eggs.

Mama was real angry with me. She was always quick to anger, but just as fast, she got over it. I, however, did not forgive that quickly. I sulked all day.

Finally, it was Christmas Eve evening. We always celebrated Christmas on Christmas Eve. We were sitting around the Christmas tree and the radio was playing Christmas music. We had no Christmas dinner, no Christmas cookies, no Christmas cake, and no presents. But Mama was right: the war was over and we had each other and we were all together again. And Mama and I were alright again with each other. We were hopeful that next year things would be better, but it actually took three years to have a somewhat normal Christmas again.

Betty Wyatt Stories

Kool Kids?

By Betty Wyatt

Timmy saw Frankie's bike inside Benson Alley. Was he back from his mother's in New York and had he not texted him yet? It had to be Frankie's. There could not be other bikes that bizarre in town, so he slipped into the alley and ducked into one of the openings, hoping not to be seen.

He spied Frankie sitting on the steps of a closed shop halfway down the Alley. He was texting someone. Timmy hardly recognized his best friend. Gone were the jeans and hoodie. He was wearing gray jeans and a sleeveless gray tee shirt. A newspaper carrier's cap covered his head. As the text ended, he took off the cap and a tumble of curls fell. His combination of shaved head and crew cut were gone.

Timmy could not believe it. He did not resemble his best friend. He was exceptionally smooth and sophisticated. When he had ended his texting, he tucked his iPhone into a jean pocket and reached in another hip pocket for a small package. He zipped it open and extracted a white cigarette that he placed between his lips. Then he pulled out a lighter and drew in a deep breath. It seemed to last forever but a huge gray cloud emerged which he blew skyward. When Tim thought that was over, a smaller cloud bubbled out. That was no cigarette. You can tell that cloud of gray was weed, hash, or marijuana, but not tobacco. Frankie's eyes were closed, and he seemed to be far away. Tim slipped from his hiding place trying to judge the new Frankie and where he, Tim Porter, would fit in with this Super Kool new Frankie Jensen.

"Don't try to slip away, Timmy boy. It's still me, with just a little wardrobe shift."

Maybe they could still be friends. Tim thought and moved closer to his best friend (he still hoped). "What's it feel like, Frankie? You look awesome."

"It feels right for me," Frankie replied and flew a cloud of smoke, causing Timmy to start coughing.

"I guess I'm still too young," Timmy said, from between coughs and gags from the pot haze.

"It's not a matter of age; you just have to figure what you need to make yourself become your version of Kool. I started with a wardrobe because that starts to mold you first. Look at what you need Tim, and then work on it. Millions of people smoke Mary Janes around the world but that doesn't make them Kool. Ask your big brother JR. He has been huffing and puffing since high school and nobody has ever called him Kool.

Tim thought that it was un-kool to cut his big brother that way. They chatted for a while and then Frankie put away his packages. "Hand me my jacket under that newspaper, Timmy-tot. Thanks for the Kaptain Kool." He pulled on a gray denim jacket that matched his pants and said, "Gotta Go Now!"

Tim sat for a few minutes thinking about what Frankie had said. Then he got up and headed home. It was almost dinnertime and he had questions. After going up to his room and doing a dab of homework, he went downstairs to his Dad's office and knocked on the door.

"Dad, I've got a problem and some questions."

"Come in Tim. I hope I have the answers you need."

Tim settled into one of the chairs by the desk. "My best friend, Frankie, is just back from New York. He spent the summer with his mom, and he is a completely changed person. He is Super Kool now,

197

has a new way of dressing, is smoking pot, and he says our JR is not yet Kool. I thought being Cum Laude in his junior year in College, receiving Athletic awards in Baseball and Soccer, plus being the lead in the Musical this summer was kool. That all looks Kool to me."

"I'd call it super smooth, Tim. As for the claim, his smoking marijuana is an old high school plague. He shook it in his sophomore year after taking a class for the summer with Dr. Clayton and me. We have continued the monitoring through his college years. You should know now that no coach at a Catholic School is going to put up with players doping and certainly, no one in the academic is going to name a user for honors in his department two years in a row. As for the musical this spring, that was just a bonus and no director is going to let a doper have a lead in his production. I think JR has been super smooth and we should be proud of him."

"I am."

"He certainly has done better than I did kicking the weed habit. I worked with Dr. Clayton in high school and all the way through Loyola. If you are thinking about taking up the habit or something stronger, you and I are going to have a chat with Dr. Clayton."

A smile appeared on his face as he looked that the story his dad was unfolding did not sound like a session with root beer and cookies.

"No, Dad, I'm not interested in taking up any kind of smoking. I just wondered what I want to be when my friends look at me. Everyone is working so hard to be Kool, I feel more drawn to your version of smooth. How do I start? I don't think a change of jeans is going to do it."

"Well, Tim, a change in wardrobe won't do much until College. Speaking of that, if you plan to go to one, you had better work on your grades now, according to that last report card. Instead of comic books, how about something more advanced? Talk it over with mom. She is a Jr. College teacher and can smooth your way. Frankie gave you one bit of good advice. Think about what you want to be in 5 years, 10 years, or 20 years. Meantime, let's just say there are folks who are working to be Kool and some who are naturally smoothly Kool."

Marketta and Geoffrey

By Betty Wyatt

Every once in a while, a Do-Gooder gets it right. Mrs. Talbot had been watching the Humane Society scoop up the Mama Cat and her six, well it was supposed to be six, but one was hiding. The Mama cat called for him, but he stayed concealed. Therefore, the crew loaded Mama and five kittens into the Mercy van, off to permanent homes in a few weeks. Mrs. Talbot felt righteous because she was the one who had called the Humane Society.

The morning had been cold and grey but now a shower came in. She watched for a few more minutes as the wind picked up and made the tree leaves dance. She saw a movement in the hedges across the street. A tiny cat had decided to make a run for it so as not to get any wetter. He guessed wrong and the skies opened and dropped buckets of water on him as he made a run for the porch of that house. A previous owner had been in a wheelchair so there was a ramp up to the low porch. He made it up and stopped to shake the water from his fur. Once on the porch he retreated to the wall. He had stopped at every step to shake his wet fur. When he got to the wall and protection from the downpour, he began to dry his fur by licking it. It was a light spray but not the soaking he had just received. There was a glider swing, which would give him shelter from the wind, and a towel was hanging from one arm of it. He pulled the towel down, dragging it under the swing, and made a nest with it. He shivered less as the towel absorbed much of the water from his pelt.

Mrs. Talbot had watched his flight to shelter and she now felt even prouder of her accomplishment in calling the Humane Society. She sang to herself as she retired to the Family Room. She made a phone call to let her friends know of her deed of the day.

The cat had fallen asleep. In an hour, the deluge eased back to a nice steady rain and the wind died down. A car pulled up and parked at the curb. The driver exited the car with an umbrella in hand and popped it open. She locked the car and then made a dash to the door of the house.

The cat burrowed deeper into the towel, but the movement caught Marketta's eyes. She ducked down to see what it was—a squirrel, a mouse, or an injured bird. She was surprised to see a tiny kitten. She laid the folded umbrella down and reached in to pull the kitten out from under the swing.

A pair of emerald eyes searched her face in fear. A human had never held her. Marketta stood up and moved to open the door, but she could not with her arms full of cat and towel, so she released the towel to let it fall. In terror, the cat clung to her. She wrapped one arm around him and began to murmur in a soft voice, "Now we are going inside and we are going to get you some warm milk and something to eat and then we are going to get you warm and dry and find you a bed to sleep in. I think I know where there is a box that will do, which has shredded paper in it. I think that was what your mother used to do."

They were in the kitchen and she reached into the fridge for the milk bottle, poured some in a pan, and then set it on the stove. All of this was new to the kitten, but he had stopped shaking on her shoulder and recognized the milk from Mrs. Talbot's treks to feed them. Now Marketta set him on the floor. Linoleum was a new experience, and he slid a bit. She set the bowl of warm milk at the base of the fridge where the warm air would comfort him.

Meanwhile she went to her bedroom to shed her own damp clothes and pulled on a warm robe and comfortable slippers. It was time to fix dinner for two, while finding out more about her new roommate.

Marketta lay awake for about an hour, planning how to raise the kitten right. She wanted to do the right thing to have a healthy, happy one. So first thing in the morning, she would call in to her work for a day off. She had not had one in ages. In the morning while she dressed, Geoffrey, as she named the cat, was having his bowl of milk. She glanced at Geoffrey who was sitting by the now empty bowl, washing his face by tongue and paw. How adorable was that? OK ready to go. She popped him into the box and carried it to the car. First stop would be the Vet. When she called last night, they said the Vet's office opened at 7:00 am. She did not make it, but a quarter to eight would do. The Vet examined the kitten, occasionally shaking his head "no's." He finally said, "He's not in bad shape, but too young to be on his own. You should board him with the Humane Society on Stevens for at least a month. They can transition his diet, box train him, and socialize him."

"They can do that?"

"It's not a common service, but with a fellow this beautiful I know they have a dozen clients who are waiting in line for him. You will have to pay for an adoption fee up front and then board a room for him. Do not lose touch with him and the last few days he is there bring in his home box and some toys that you take home with him. Maybe your slippers, too, so you will smell right to him."

So, it was off to the S.V. Humane Society to pay the adoption fee, get papers of ownership, photos, and getting Geoffrey his strictly temporary tag. She visited him every day on her lunch break.

Going home day finally came and they seemed mutually happy to share the ride home to the house he would soon think of as his. She had problems balancing work and home life, so she asked her Boss if she could bring him to the studio office.

"Sure, why not? We'll give it a try," Antonio grinned. One day at work, Geoffrey was up on the desk and made a paw print design on a roll of paper on her worktable. Antonio loved it and put it in production at once.

She produced a Cat Pajamas in Linen and silk that made it to Vogue, a first for the company. She is now working on a toddler ware to be called, "Cozy Kitten." She is no longer lonely and has the best of living. That is the "Cat's Meow" in achievement.

School Days Golden Rule Day
By Betty Wyatt

It had been twenty plus years since she had been on a campus. Memories of those years when she matriculated at UCLA came flooding back, but there was no resemblance to this campus. This was San Jose State and it had preceded her old Alma Mater by decades and had largely been rebuilt using concrete blocks.

She was returning to school to try to avoid the fate that was overtaking a neighbor in her cul-de-sac, Gwen Johnson. Gwen had always left everything up to Walter, her very successful husband, she thought. She had never worked a day in her life. Walter had suddenly died and the fortune she had always assumed was in the bank or in a trust was nowhere. His financial records showed that he had spent every dime he made and the gifts he showered on his wife with were her inheritance. Even the house was mortgaged and would have to be sold. She had no marketable skills except a good voice. Maybe she could find an agent and do voice commercials.

Well, maybe.

Fortunately, for me, Laura Robins, a third cul-de-sac neighbor, still works in the Registrar's office of SJS. She and I had been conferring about how practical it would be for me to go back to school and get that old Masters finished, and get a teaching credential for high school or junior college.

I had picked up all the official papers an hour ago and was now seated in the graduate students' cafeteria on campus with a cup of coffee and in a state of shock.

When I did my work on my masters, it was with our Dr. Phelan, a 1900 resident of Central America and a secret agent for the Navy. It had only been a single investigation for him. With the burgeoning enrollments in the intervening years, there were a dozen or more Masters for him to review so it now was off limits for Masters. All my work was down the drain, though it is still out there. Dr. Hudson had kept my preliminary study and filed it in his records where graduates soon picked it dry. Well, we will skip the Masters anyway.

I flipped through the other pages. Although my old Alma Mater ranks higher than my possible current one, the cost here is much higher than I paid in the University—so many waker uppers. Laura also pointed out that there was no Graduate Records Exam scheduled until mid-terms. Therefore, there was no chance for a scholarship until next term.

Laura plunked down in the seat next to me. "You're looking distressed," she observed.

Well, it is more complicated than I thought it would be. I thank you for all the work you did on this. Can I bring you a cup of coffee and a piece of pie in partial payment?"

"Make it apple and you've got a deal. The server took their order and the rest of the session ended in neighborhood chatter.

Woes of the Working Woman
By Betty Wyatt

Twila had never felt so tired. The empty parking space in front of her apartment was the answer to her prayers. She slid out of the Porsche after checking the latches on the top. Someone had tried to pry it open the last time she parked on the street. Then, moving to the back of the car, she opened the trunk and began putting all of the stuff into a big canvas tote bag.

It weighed a ton. She locked the trunk and tried to hoist the loaded tote up the curb. Two tugs and she knew she was not going to make it, but her guardian angel must have been working overtime that night. Neighbor Charlie was just coming into view from the Bar down the street. He was made of muscle.

"Hi, Charlie," she chortled. "Care to do a good deed for the day? I can't hoist this tote up to the sidewalk."

"Sure, Red, anything for a damsel in distress."

He stepped off the curb and lifted the bag as if it were nothing. "Now what?" he queried.

"I need to get into the elevator and up to the third floor of my apartment."

"Small task to undertake for one who is such a good cook."

"I'm not playing cook tonight, Charlie. This is all homework for tonight, but I'll give you either Italian or Chinese for Sunday!"

"Done!" he said, hoisting the tote and striding into the lobby. Twila trotted after him, ignoring the mailbox when she passed it.

She had her keys out when they reached the door and opened it, so he could walk into the foyer. He set the load down beyond the foyer table, outside of her office door. She took his hands and kissed them both to make the welts more comfortable. "Do you want to bring a guest Sunday Night, and which do you prefer—Chinese or Italian?"

He licked his lips once and said, "Chinese, Red, my heart's desire."

She turned him toward the door and patted him on the back to start him moving through the door. "Now I must turn that tote bag's contents into dialogue, and write two business programs."

She turned on the coffee maker and then turned to the fridge to grab an energy drink. She drank it while her dinner cooked in the microwave. While everything was simmering and perking, she went to her bedroom to hang up her coat, kick off her heels, and slip into ballerina slippers. Then back to the kitchen with a detour through the bathroom. She dished up the dinner, warmed a roll in the microwave, and took some ready-made slaw from the fridge. She dissolved onto the armed kitchen nook chair and finally, relaxing, she ate her dinner leisurely. She had asked Google for some soft music and it was serenading her. She closed her eyes, and pretended she was in a restaurant and she smiled.

She rinsed the dishes and stacked them in the sink to be washed later on by the dishwasher. The first business program went easily. It would start with an introductory 2-training program, which Harriet and her boss were laying out tonight. This was followed by a week in which the group was split up to work in local branches to test the techniques. Friday and Saturday were for more testing and discussion. She finished the sample tests of the techniques and a summary of hopes. In a month, the trainees would take a test she would write during the month to judge the effectiveness of the program. The second program was an in-office experiment that would involve some role-playing by employees and members of a local theater group. People would have scripts they had to memorize and play. It was fun to write. Sometimes it was employees, sometimes clients, and other times customers. They had not decided on the number of employees who will participate.

It was now midnight. She did not have an ounce of energy left in her body, nor an idea in her brain. It was bedtime. So she got up from the computer, turned out the light, and went to her bedroom She undressed, just throwing her clothes over the footboard, donning her gown, and slipping into bed, after setting her alarm for 3:00 am.

Sometimes when you are too tired, it is hard to fall asleep, but she was out as if she was being drugged. At 3:00 am, she groaned as she emerged from the covers. She pulled on her robe and slippers and headed to the bathroom to splash some cold water on her face and take a morning pill a little early. She had drained the coffee pot into the thermos before going to bed and now had a cup from it.

In the computer room, she opened the Little Theater Box and set up the Pop-Up Miniature Theatre. It was a two-story set. She got out her timing materials and a video of a rehearsal and began covering the actions of the latest rehearsal.

Deep in concentration, she did not hear the light tap at her door, but she heard the loud banging when it began. She went to the door, making sure it was on the chain before she opened it a crack.

"Oh, there you are," a drunken voice shouted. She opened the door a bit more, keeping it on the chain.

"Charlie, why are you here at this hour?"

"They closed the Bar and told us all to go home, and I believe this is where my home should be, here with you, my red-tressed Twila."

"Charlie, I'm tired and I'm working, so go home."

"I told you this is my real home."

She had opened the door a little bit more on the chain for a better look at his condition. His clothes were rumpled, and his shirt was stained as if he had spilled a drink on it. "Oh, dear."

"Open the door," and he gave it a push, popping the chain latch off the door and she struggled to latch it again. That only caused him to back up and make a run for it. The door crashed inward, spinning her to the floor. The door had caught her in the right side as it hit her, and she could feel a sharp pain as she passed out.

Confused by the result of what he had done, Charlie picked her up and carried her out of the dark apartment and into the illuminated hall. He tried to wake her but she remained unconscious, so he shook her. Then, leaning over her he yelled, "Twila, Twila, wake up. This is no time to sleep."

As he set back on his heels, he began to cry. "Please God, wake her up. I did not mean to hurt her. I just wanted to hold her gently in my arms." He then bent over her body, rocking back and forth from his kneeling position, in order to support her by his arms.

After a few minutes, her eyelids fluttered, and she stirred. He straightened up and began to smile through his tears. She spoke, "Get up, and get your phone and call an ambulance. It's hard to breath and I hurt my chest."

"I can't use my phone. I left it on the counter at the bar."

She pushed the button on her emergency necklace and yelled "Help" as loud as she could. They must have heard the door being shattered. Why didn't any of her neighbors appear to help? This time she screamed again and repeated it as soon as she could breathe. Charlie was now leaning over her again. His pants were soaked in something and it didn't smell like urine. It covered her left side and she continued to scream for help.

Since Charlie was hanging over her, he did not see or hear Twila's across the hall neighbor open her door and step toward the room. Mrs. Rosencrantz was clutching a large rolling pin, and stepped quickly beside Charlie. Recapturing the swing from when she was a pro-golfer, she whacked Charlie's head! The force of her blow caused him to collapse and fall clear of Twila, onto his left shoulder, thus freeing Twila's body. Standing erect and still holding the rolling pin dripping blood, Mrs. Rosencrantz yelled, "You can all come out now, you sniveling cowards. She is your neighbor and needed help. He's unconscious now and should be out for a while." Moreover, she strode erect into her apartment. The neighbors had called 911, some for Police help, and another for an ambulance. He left his phone number and address, and the fourth went to the local Round-the-Clock News Station and he reported he had film of most of the action.

The first to arrive were the two beat cops who could not believe. It was sweet kind Charlie Walker, and they ordered a police ambulance for Charlie. Next were the Station Police Officers and various Techs. A civilian ambulance arrived for Twila but one of the cops had already ordered a special tech ambulance from the investigation branch to transport Twila to the lab to examine her for suspected Rape.

During this portion of the operation, one of the Cops was heard to ask, "Which one of you laid Charlie out like this?" No one spoke up, but Mrs. Rosencrantz who had been listening behind her door, stepped out and said, "I solved the problem, and this is the weapon." Handing a sergeant the rolling pin, the sergeant looked startled to see a skinny old woman in her 70's being the wielder of the weapon.

The First of a Long Year Friendship

By Betty Wyatt

He was a gift of Love and his arrival was the beginning of an extraordinary relationship. It was Bobby Archer's 7th birthday. His mother, Ruth, had invited seven of Bobby's friends to celebrate. The party started in the Archer's Family Room. You know the Archer's home, that tall house with the dog weather vane at the top of the hill where Ambling Road ends. It is a house that shows its years, but it was Jim's granddad's home, and they love it. When Jim gets his promised raise next year, they will start some restoration.

Meantime the boys were playing the usual birthday games that kids play, and then Ruth brought in the ice cream and cake. The candles were blown out and they fell upon the feasting and began opening gifts. Bobby finished opening his gifts, which ranged from a pair of boots from grandmother, TV games, and Trekkie movies for his computer. Dad walked in with a cardboard box holding a wiggly cargo. It was not wrapped, but it barked. The boys surrounded it and as Jim took his hand off the top, a head emerged of a 9-week-old Airedale puppy. He tipped the box and the puppy stepped out. Bobby gathered him up in his arms and proclaimed, "This is the best gift I've ever gotten, ever!" Since he had a bit of ice cream on his face, the lick he got from the puppy was a great slurpy wet lick that sealed their bond.

"What is his name, Dad?"

"I don't know, Bob, that's up to you?" Several suggestions came from the other boys. Rodger, the oldest boy said, "We asked our dog what his name was, and he said Woof, so he's been Woof for ten years."

"Good idea!" Bobby said. "What's your name, Dog?" The wiggling pup looked up at him and said, "Arfer."

"Wonderful. We'll name him for Uncle Arthur." Dad and Mom broke into laughter. Uncle Arthur was mom's 18-year-old kid brother and a football scholarship student at USC in Los Angeles. Bobby thought he was the coolest grown-up he knew. When you are just turning seven, an 18-year-old football player who won an All-State award from high school when he graduated, as an adult is your hero.

Three Lessons in One Day

By Betty Wyatt

Paul's hand squeezed the tomato in his jacket pocket, hoping to make it soften up a little. It was hard as a rock. He wanted it splashy. He walked faster as he spotted three other students ahead of him, probably headed to the same place. However, even if he caught up with them, they would not ask him to join them. These were the Guys—John, George, and Rap' Ray. They had the "Stuff." They were Guys; he was just one of the boys at school.

They were all headed toward a Saturday Protest about Vietnam. It was a big deal. A National Senator was speaking on why the U.S. and China should agree to a United Nations request that they both withdraw troops from Vietnam and let the two native populations settle their own dispute. It had been the table topic between Paul's grandfather, a Full Colonel in WW2, and Paul's dad, a Major from the Korean War—both West Pointers.

In addition to rolling the tomato around in his pocket, Paul was rolling around the discussion in his head. He knew his family was hoping he would get an appointment to one of the Military Academies. He was not sure he wanted that and he was chafing at taking Latin in the last year of Middle School. It was required by West Point and the Air Academy. Right now, he was tackling Caesar'. What relevancy did that have today?

As he turned the corner and entered the parking lot at the end of First Street, he could see several hundred people gathered with banners, and flags of various nations, including China and Nam. They were just beginning to get the mass into some sort of order for the rally-march. The monitors were moving the participants into lines of ten across and ten lines per unit with a monitor for each. He laughed. Here was Julius Caesar' Centurions. It ended up with five blocks of phalanxes of 100 each and then a motley group at the end of 40 or 50 people. Late comers would be added to their ranks.

There was not a full band leading the groups—only a couple of drummers, some bugles, and two pipes. This was kind of a sad attempt in keeping the beat, making it into a march.

They went up First Street to the Park at the Court House. A stage was set up in the middle of the park with chairs, speaker's podium, and the back of the stage held an array of American flags, with the foreign flags at each end. The marchers were very neat and fell into their places well. Paul was impressed and he could see his three schoolmates were still with the group. He thought anything so organized might have driven them off. The three prided themselves in being rebels.

The mayor introduced the Senator from Washington, D.C. and he began to speak. He pointed out that we were honored to have a number of veterans joining the programs. Curtains opened at one end of the stage and six wounded vets, two in wheel chairs, and the rest walking, joined the assembly and took their seats near the podium.

About ten minutes into his address, the Senator summoned a Sergeant with one arm to the podium and asked him about his wound, and where he got it. As the Sergeant began to speak, a tomato flew from the ranks where Paul was standing and he believed it to come from John. There was a gasp from the ranks of marchers and the many curiosity seekers who had joined the listeners. The tomato smashed on the soldiers' shoulder and trickled down his shirt through the array of ribbons on his chest.

Paul was shocked. This was wrong. This was very wrong. This man had honorably served his country. He fought to defend freedom of speech and he was being publicly humiliated. The sergeant who was the target ignored the assault, except for flinching when the tomato struck him. He answered the Senator's question and both kept their cool. Another of the wounded men was called forward, and this time a flurry of tomatoes flew to the stage, amid shouts from the crowd. Then men and women in the ranks began to throw their fruit at those throwing tomatoes at the six G.I.'s. The ranks broke and then throws from the ranks hit the row of flags and they toppled one by one onto the floor.

The police were now arriving and began to try to bring order back to the ranks, but it was impossible. Paul had not moved from his place, but when the flags fell, it was the final straw for him and he dropped out of the ranks and fled to the opposite end of the park, where all was surprisingly calm. He sat down on a bench with his elbows on knees, and head in hands, he tried to figure it out. How could anything go so wrong, so quick? He raised his head from his hands and looked back at what had turned into a riot. Additional cops were arriving and a fire truck pulled up and attached hoses to the hydrants. At a signal from the cops, they began to pressure the crowd with the hoses. This broke up the fierce fighting and the crowd began running and leaving the park. The police officers were stopping many and placing them under arrest.

Frustrated, confused, disappointed, Paul took his big tomato out of his pocket and taking aim at a big sycamore, in anger hurled it at the tree. It splashed very nicely on the white trunk of the trees. As the juices ran down the trunk, two squirrels scampered down to sip the juice and followed it to the ground where they consumed the tomato remains. He laughed again. Pleased with the result of his weapon, he took one of the smaller ones from his pocket and hurled it at the tree. The squirrels had scampered up the tree and were not hit, but came back at once to feed.

Then a surprise. A raccoon emerged from the clump of bushes beside the tree and joined the squirrels in slurping up the tomato. Paul leaned back on the bench in pleasure at the sight, and he grinned from ear to ear.

"What are you so happy about?" he hears, and he saw Rap' Ray standing there. "I can't see anything myself to be happy about on this disastrous day."

"I'm happy about how I used my weapons today to feed the squirrel and raccoon. I am pleased that I have never seen a raccoon before and never expected to see one in a City Park. I am glad I did not commit a morally indefensible act by dishonoring a hero. And, I'm glad I found relevance in the 230th Century for 2,000 year old writings of Julius Caesar."

I wish I had been with you, Paul. John is on his way to the hospital after a member of the audience who turned out to be a Stanford lineman, beat him up for dishonoring a wounded soldier. George is on his way to jail for assaulting a cop. I feel like a coward for sneaking away from the riot."

Did you dishonor yourself by dishonoring one of the Soldiers or the Senator? Did you soil and topple the flags. Did you hurt anybody in the crowd?"

"No. The only tomato I threw didn't even reach the stage. I wouldn't let George and John sing the Disparaging Rap I had written. I was ashamed of it when I noticed the way the crowd was acting. I didn't think it was going to be like that. I thought the folks really wanted to hear what the Senator had to say and hear him explain what the compromise suggestion was."

"Got any tomatoes left?"

"Just two small ones."

"Let's get that raccoon back out if we can." And he took the tomatoes from Ray and they both sat quietly on the bench as he tossed one tomato that drew the squirrels and the other one that brought the raccoon back.

"Any day you can convert a weapon into a treat, is a good day."

From Blues to Cheers

By Betty Wyatt

It had been raining all day. The view out her window was very depressing. The trees were drooping, with no bird activity at the feeders. Her mind was just as empty as the streets. Is this what people used to call the blues? Mary Jo did not see anything to sing about.

Tomorrow is my birthday—my 90th Birthday. What is there to look forward to on a 90th birthday?

She drew the drapes to shut out the depressing blues thoughts. Substituting the even more downing of the early evening news, there were more shootings in Oakland and one in the City.

She went into the kitchen, popped a frozen entre into the microwave, and made a salad while it cooked. Another dinner alone. How she missed Robert, her husband of 50 years, mostly at these familiar two-some activities.

She decided a bath might lift her spirits. She filled the tub to soaking level and just relaxed every muscle in her body. A half hour soak seemed to perk her up and she got out of the tub, dried, slipped into her pajamas and walked into the bedroom and slipped into the bed. Thanks to the napoleon, she slept like a weary dog. She probably snored, but there was no one to hear, so it did not matter.

She breakfasted and dressed in a colorful suit. After all, she should look festive even if no one knew it. At the lobby desk, she was stunned to find a lovely bouquet of yellow and red roses. The card just said from your "Fan Club." Who could that be? Was it just a joke?

When she got to the first class at the Senior Center, she found three Happy Birthday balloons. She smiled and said thank you to those assembled, who smiled and sort of cheered. The flowers arrived from the front desk and the messenger set them on the podium.

Three classmates joined, but no one was as old as she was today. They began to chat and this became a question from one of the groups, and an answer from Mary Jo. They knew she had been a writer, but not much else. It came out that she had worked for Vogue and so the questions flowed out. Asking about celebrities she had known, and back room tales about Fashion Shows and Photo Shoots.

She was happy, she suddenly realized. Talking about yesterday and the good life she had held for so many years, brought back those days and those feelings. At the end of the hour as they were supposed to disperse, the two young women she had been working with here on a work of fiction she started forty years ago, but never finished, came in.

One of the girls had sent the partial note to a publisher and he had ordered them to finish it, which they had been doing for several months. They had not worked on it for the last month because they had sent the manuscript to the publisher and were awaiting comment.

The two girls who have been helping her, Milly and Susan, were hiding something in a tote bag, but first came a birthday coffee with a birthday cake. Then holding an iPhone, which she withdrew from the tote, Milly turned it on to *"Pomp and Circumstance."*

Susan was throwing papers out of the Tote, and finally brought forth a wrapped package to Mary Jo. She began unwrapping it until the final red, white, and blue wrapping fell to the floor. She gazed at the book in her hands and began to cry.

Murmuring, "Oh my God, oh my God, this is the happiest day of my life. How did you do it?"

Milly replied, "We pointed out to Mr. Bloomster and the Editor for fiction, Thomas Blanding, that you were 90 Years old, and would love to see something from your early works published before you depart this earth. Mr. Bloomster was surprised to find out that you are 90 years old."

Susan, who always likes to be correct in her statements said, "At the time Mary Jo was only 89 years old, she said you can't do a book in that time, but you can do something that shows it's in the works."

Milly broke in. "Mr. Bloomster just laughed and said, "Who says we can't get a limited edition out in six weeks? We did it during the war all the time. An edition of 300 will be ready for the June Book Show to let book sellers know what is on the fall lists. How's that for a birthday present?" And this is the dummy copy for you to have today from Mr. Bloomster."

The whole room was cheering, and the director came down from his office to see what was going on. He had one of the maintenance men bring down the cart that the director used to tour the layout. The balloons were tied to it.

The director drove and Mrs. Mary Jo Thorn and her Book toured the Building. P.R. had been on the phone and TV camera men ended the ride, along with the story for the 9:00 News.

And that was the Happiest day of Mary Jo's life.

Fast Friends

By Betty Wyatt

The line was unbelievably long. The day sweat was dripping hot and here Gerry was standing in line carrying two totes that weighed a ton. Why hadn't she come here first? Her mask was slipping on her chin. This stupid COVID19 had turned her life around, and made every day become a series of disasters. Ten more people to go in the line. She steeled herself. Yes, she would make it.

The man in line behind her seemed downright comfortable. She decided to hate him. He was wearing a Panama hat, a tank top, and Bermuda shorts with canvas shoes, but no socks. Why couldn't women dress like that? Well they could if they were going to work in the yard but were not going out in public. Maybe he was one of the homeless she was always seeing on late night TV. Then he lifted his left arm to check his watch—it was a Rolex. No homeless here.

If only she could set these totes down. Her arms felt as though they were pulling out of their sockets. Oh dear, Oh God the multiple pains. It was all getting to her. She felt herself swaying and then she blacked out.

When she opened her eyes, it was to a dizzy world. The man behind her was now lifting her to sip some ice water. She groaned. "What happened?"

Someone in the crowd that surrounded her said, "You blacked out, honey, but I've got your totes. Some smart alley kid tried to snatch your totes, but they are right here, and we also saved your place in line for you."

It's Don's turn now. "That's me," the man behind her said, and then it's your turn. Let's see if you can sit. Taylor is headed home, so she is lending you her walker for the totes. I have her address and we can drop it off when taking you home. Unless you want to go to the hospital, I can do that, too."

"Are you sure I can still get the test after passing out?"

"The Doc said so. He said it was just some stress and a lot of heat."

"You are going to live," he grinned. He helped her up and he placed her onto the walker.

Carrying the totes, a dusky skinned young woman said, "I'll just lug these to the car for you, honey."

"You've all been so kind. How can I thank you?"

An old timer in the back shouted, "Vote for Joe, and stay well." That brought a big laugh from the mini crowd around her and from the folks standing in line.

After waiting over two hours in line, the swab test took only 2 minutes. Don stepped up to push the walker and said, "I was so relieved to hear you were Miss Hopper, Gerry. I was so afraid it would be Mrs. I am also single and unattached; now lets hear from your other new friend.

"Who me?" The tote totter said with the big smile. I'm Maryland Smith, but you can call me Mary. We work in the same building as Miss Gerry. Only she's upstairs and I'm down in the coffee shop.

"I'm sorry Mary, I didn't recognize you out of your uniform."

"Where are you going, Don?"

"I thought I might as well put the car away for the night when I came down for my COVID19 test since the garage is right here."

"But, this is the garage for my building."

Don grinned at her. "Mine, too."

The Mercedes slipped smoothly down the ramp and into the number 4 slot, which was protected on each side. As they prepared to emerge from the car, he asked her if she felt up to walking, or did she need the walker.

"I'm sure I can still walk without it."

They entered the elevator and exited at her floor—No. 3. He walked her to her door carrying the totes and set them down on the floor. He turned to get her key and opened the door. Then he reached inside to turn on the light switch. She gave him a puzzled look. "How did you know that?"

"They're all like that in this building."

"Don, you've been so helpful today."

"I still wish we had taken you to see your doctor. Are you sure you're all right?" He leaned against the door.

"I'm feeling OK. I'll take a Tylenol and get some sleep."

"Then you can pay me back by coming to dinner tomorrow night. You pick the time and I'll pick the place. How's that sound? If you have any problems tonight, here is my phone. I can be here in ten minutes. It's not by magic. I'm just upstairs."

He had been holding her hand as they said good night and now he lifted it and kissed it. Thank you.

And so it began....

A Too Familiar Feeling

By Betty Wyatt

K.D. ran down the iron steps from the elevated platform and delighted in the sprawled out metropolis spread before him. He had only been here for three months and the contrast to his Texas town squeezed along the Rio Grande's border with Mexico among the Resacas was exciting. He had grown up in Brownsville as Kenny Dahl Smithson, which the kids turned into Kenny Doll, which made his life miserable. He was short which made it worse. Therefore, he solved the problem by taking up wrestling, and then judo, while taking the name K.D.

Chicago was a metropolis with a Great Lake in its front yard. This part of the city was all business. The shopping center and "Downtown" were several blocks south and east. From the staircase, he could see a dozen corporate headquarters and looming among them was the Wilshire Amalgamated Holdings. A 14-story tower with shining steel girders decorating it thrusting into the skies. Our own office was much closer in. A five-story building with a marble facade rose gracefully among its neighbors, with many of the top floor's offices having balconies and landscaped terraces with trees on the roof.

K.D reached the entry to his building and glanced at the bronze lacquer set on the marble facing: FAIRFAX PUBLISHERS, in bold polished print and below that in small letters, a WILSHIRE HOLDING. He entered the building and walked to the elevators, which were swiftly distributing the waiting employees. The fashion Quarterlies at the second floor, his own Nature publication on the third floor, and Sports on the fourth.

His phone rang just as he was entering an elevator, so he withdrew to take the call. "Ken Smithson," he answered.

"Mr. Smithson, this is Dr. Gorgon's office. He would like you to come to his office at 3:00 this afternoon and bring your portfolio of articles you have completed for us. Take Elevator B from your floor to our office." The voice was cold, and she hung up.

"Oh God, what had he done? He recognized the cold feeling of panic. He had been called to the Principal's office more than once, and the feeling is here again.

His blithe spirit was gone. He entered the elevator and walked slowly to his desk. He answered the calls on his desk phone but none of them gave a clue to his question, "Why was he being summoned to the publisher's office, and what did it mean?"

What did "Bring your portfolio mean?" He just kept his completed articles in his computer with a copy in a file drawer, with any relevant comments about it made after publication. He sees John, Long fellow, the publisher, and editor of the Nature Quarterlies. As usual, the elderly gentleman's door was open for all to wander in. The rest of their suite was very contemporary in feel, but John's office was early 20th century. Couches, comfortable chairs, paintings on the wall, bookcases full of bound Quarterlies, and reference materials as well as books they had published. It was homey and Ken always enjoyed poking around in it.

John waved him to a seat by the desk. "What is the worried look, K.D? Your article was top. Good writing, good research, bound to get a reaction."

"It has. I'm summoned upstairs to meet Dr. Gorgon, with my portfolio. What's my portfolio?"

"Oh, didn't we go over that when you started?"

"If we did, I've forgotten it."

"I'll send Sally over to help you. She's done it many times."

Then he swiveled his chair to face Ken. "When you were in your training program, you were given a large book outlining WILSHIRE HOLDINGS, right? Did you study it?"

"Yes, I got it. Did I study it? No, I flipped through it stunned at the number of companies they control, but I couldn't see how that affected me here at Fairfax."

I'm sorry Ken. I knew Gunther was a Holding and did not warn you. I have wanted to retire for 5 years but they wouldn't let me. Now they make me retire. I get full pension and benefits and I think my 4:00 appointment will be my forced retirement. I used you and that is unforgiveable, but I think it will be worth your while. Just hold steady and do not panic. You are a good writer and you made a great impression on the staff here. We'll work it out."

Ken left the office confused. His article was true, the research he cited impeccable. Wouldn't Wilshire want to clear up the mess? Wouldn't it be a public relations boon for them? What had he done wrong?

Sally put together the folders in his drawer and found two nice covers for them. He set off for Elevator B and his fate at 2:45. The elevator opened directly into Dr. Gorgon's office and his cold-eyed reception mirrored his Secretary's. When Ken was seated, the Doctor reached for the portfolios. He flipped through them nodding yes, from time to time. You're a fine writer Mr. Smithson, but you bit the hand that feeds you when you took on a Wilcox Holding. We do not criticize any of their Holdings. It's their Golden Rule."

"But Dr. Gorgon, it could be such a P.I. advantage to clean up an internal problem before the Dept. of Agriculture attacks them. Today, improving the environment in any measure is a boon to be hailed and celebrated. They must have labs that have been working on new products. They had to know this was coming. I focused on the beloved bird, Bobolink, because it appeals to millions of citizens, but the damage is real for livestock and is costing farmers thousands of dollars and poisoning breeding stock. They must see this. They know their market. That red headed kid with the freckles extolling their products is on hundreds of barns and billboards. Surely they want to keep him as a happy symbol of their friendship with farmers."

"I agree with you Kenneth, but it's worth my job and possibly Fairfax's existence."

"How many other Holdings do they have that may be environmental or climate control problems. They have got to attack them before the politician's get hold of the information. If they are solving the problem internally, it will save them. They must see that," Ken countered.

"What was the lab that did the research? You protected them with a pseudonym."

"I can't tell you that without their permission, Dr. Gorgon. It is valid, but their grants and funds could be pulled if the wrong people get a hold of it before Wilshire starts a well-publicized clean up. Can't they buy a smaller company with a clean product for a start?" The secretary appeared at the end of the room.

"I'm sorry to interrupt but your 4:00 appointment is here."

"Thank you, Millicent. Ken, I want you to go with me when I meet with the Holdings at Wilshire on Monday. Can you wait until this appointment is over?" and K.D. nods yes.

"Millicent, show Mr. Smithson into the green room and get him some coffee and a snack. This should not take long, but see that he is comfortable. Don't forget these," he said, extending the portfolios.

K.D. followed Millicent out of the room. He wondered if his trip to the principal's office was over yet. If he is fired why should he go with Dr. Gorgon to the heads of Holdings meeting on Monday? Was there still a future for him with Fairfax?

Jason Writes a Letter

By Betty Wyatt

Jenna and her 10-year-old son were sprawled on the couch in the family room watching an old Van Johnson movie in which he was saving the world in WW2. Jason projected Van Johnson's smiling good looks onto his Jet flying father in Asia.

"Mom, do you think the President could bring Dad home for Christmas?"

"Christmas? We just had Christmas a couple of months ago. Why not the 4th of July or Easter, if you are lonesome to see him?"

"It's not like that. I was just thinking. This will be our last one together. The girls graduate this June and are shooting for scholarships. It was so keen this year having most of the family together. Your mom and dad were here, and we went to visit Dad's Mother at the Senior Living place and Santa showed up. We were all there except for Dad. It was so great."

Thinking of those 10 days, Jenna leaned her head back on the sofa cushions to blink back the tears.

"He says he's the most powerful man in the world but I'm not sure that moving individual servicemen around is part of his assignment. You could always write him a letter, I guess. There's an awful lot of protocol to cover."

"Where should I send it? To the Air Force?"

"No, that's the easy part. Mail to the President goes to the White House. Like all citizens, he gets mail at his home," mom said. For two weeks, the ten-year-old labored on the letter up in his room.

On Valentine's Day, he presented it to mom at breakfast. She was amazed. It looked as though it had been typed in an office by a pro. "How did you do this, darling?"

"Well, first I asked Google and then I asked Mrs. Thorne, my last year's teacher for help. I remembered that she used to talk a lot about being a White House page."

"I think it will do the job and get to the President. You explained you had help on the format, but the details are all from you. All you need to do now is sign it."

He had been practicing different signatures and his mother picked out a simple readable one, not one of the fancy ones that Jason preferred. So it was finally stamped, and as Jason headed off to school, Jenna headed to the Post Office.

Every day he dashed home from School, but no reply. Then one April Saturday as Jason was getting ready to go to soccer practice his mother called up the stairs. "Jason, you have a visitor." Glancing out the window at the head of the stairs, he was stunned to see a Jeep, with a driver in uniform, sitting at the curb.

He stumbled a bit with nerves on the stairway but steadied himself as he walked into the living room. An Air Force Captain rose from the couch and came forward to introduce himself. Jason did not know whether to salute or take his hand but did the latter and spoke crisply to the Captain's questions. Jenna appeared with a tray with coffee and coffee cake. She invited the two to be seated on the couch and have the coffee. She took a seat in one of the chairs that flanked the couch. The Captain, David Farrell, explained that the letter had been widely circulated from White House to Public Relations, and finally back to the White House, where the President eventually saw it.

"You haven't yet verified if it is a legitimate request. So, I am here to verify that you are the 10-year-old son of a combat pilot in Afghanistan."

This was the first time the family learned of where he was assigned. Now they had sent Captain Farrell to identify the boy.

Jason grinned as he stood before the Captain. Here is a ten-year-old son of a Combat pilot in Asia. Turning to his seated mom, "Am I your son? And is my dad stationed in Asia?"

His mother smiled and replied. "I need to go to the bank to the safety deposit to get your Birth certificate, but if Captain Farrell will accept my word for it, you are truly my only ten-year-old son and I witnessed you writing a letter to the President."

Captain Farrell sat down on the couch and motioned for Jason to join him. He opened a small pocket notebook, and the two of them began chatting. Jenna rose to leave, but Jason and the Captain asked her to stay.

The interview lasted about a half hour. The Captain thanked Jenna for the coffee and pastry, and Jason for his cooperation. "I will be in contact from time to time, Jason, if that is OK with you, and Mrs. Taylor?"

"That's fine with me and I'm sure it will be OK with Jason."

From to time, Captain Farrell dropped by to chat and told Jason he had been in contact with his dad a couple of times. After June, the visits became fewer as the long summer dragged on, and Jason stopped checking the mailbox on his way home from soccer. An occasional visit from Captain Farrell was the only bright spot.

Then, in November, while Jason was in class, his mom checked the mailbox. It was mostly ads of course. Thanksgiving was coming and the great annual shopping fest was just around the corner. In among the stuff was a stiff white envelope with a small depiction of the White House on the upper left corner of its fine vellum surface. It was addressed "To be opened only by Jason Taylor."

Only by coincidence, Captain Farrell had dropped by for a tea and chat, since it was time for school to be out. The Captain got into his car and headed the mile to the school. Jason was with his group soccering down the street on a long trip home.

Jason gets into the car, "There's a letter from the white house for you. It is addressed to you so no one else can open it. This is it, Jason, Captain Farrell said.

Jason ran from the car to the door, which his mother was holding open, waving a white vellum envelope. "I think you had better sit down and read whatever it says, Jason." Jason's face wore a worried look as he walked up the steps to take the letter from his mother. When she handed it to him, he studied it for several seconds—The White House in the corner, with his name. Then he started to rip it open, but a sharp call came from Jenna. "No! Don't tear it," as she handed him a letter opener.

He carefully inserted the opener under the flap and extracted a single sheet of vellum. Passing the envelope to his mother, he began to read the letter to himself. The worried look relaxed and slowly became a grin as he read on. The President could not extend a serving service man's term. Then came a smile as he read his dads term of over-seas service was over and he would be transferred to the states on November 12th and it was already the 11th. He restrained an impulse to dance and jubilantly passed the letter to his mother who read it aloud to the group that had assembled. They had assumed from his expressions, that there was good news. There were tears and cheers as she finished the letter. DAD WOULD BE HOME BY THANKSGIVING! Jason was wrapped in Jenna's arms as the group celebrated and dispersed.

Covid Memories

By Betty Wyatt

Having finished their regular Friday afternoon of golf, the four men were seated at a picnic table next to the parking lot at the Municipal Woods Hole Golf Course. It was a popular spot, and they were lucky to have a table on the edge of the lawn. It swept over the rolling coastal hills toward the bay with many boats sailing by. The far edge of the Bay was beach backed by its wetland of reeds, which was headed by the East Bay Regional Parkland California, which was very charming.

The eldest man was first to speak after setting down his beer that had come from the ice chest at the end of the table. The others were still working on theirs. "Now that its 15 years behind us, what are your memories or feelings about the disastrous pandemic that took over our lives for two years?"

With a big grin on his face, one black man (yes, we call them black these days) raised his hand. "Let me answer that because I probably have a different view of it. We call it the great leveler. The Black Demonstrations of the preceding decade had rattled the doors on the years of segregation and all of its suppression pressures. We didn't have a higher rate of disease than you did," he said, motioning to the white men. Turning to the Latino Pero Amado, "Your people did that, Pedro, and it must have been beyond painful to every family in your Spanish towns. But this time the virus hit just as hard on the whites as it did the people of color. We both went through periods of economic devastation. We had the virus, but you had it just as bad and the white nurses in the hospital treated us just as well as they did to you. Likewise, our health workers were just as passionate in their care for you. The economic aids were handed out more fairly than ever before. Checks came to us and to Asians and to Latinos, as well as to you.

"I would not have been part of your group 20 years ago and I certainly would not have been able to play on this course or drive that car," as he jerked a finger to point to a new Benz. None of this was said in a negative way. He was grinning and raising his brow to toast the gains.

His friends laughed at some of his points and shook their heads at his conclusions in telling his side of COVID-19.

Cart, the older man who threw out the first challenge, said, "Who's next?" Red said, "Okay, my memories are somewhat different. My family had a successful chain of small Menswear stores. You can imagine what happened to us. We got no help at all until almost the end of the financial crash. My brother got Covid-21, the second version of the virus, and was in the hospital for a month. He came out with destroyed lungs, and has been on oxygen therapy ever since. He has become a musician and composer of serious classical music. He was a part of a PBS show called The Survivors. His quartet provides the music for interviews with people like us. I, therefore, have had to try to rebuild his business, with Dad's help. We lost our big house but managed to buy one of the new ones, and in truth, it is more comfortable and convenient than that old gothic monster. You might remember it. It stood where the new Kohl's is now. I guess like you, Jason, we are better off, but it has been so hard on my folks. Mother is in treatment for a mental problem, my kid sister lost a baby during the Epidemic, and she switched careers from teaching preschool to Nursing. Her husband left her and moved to Nevada. They are now divorced. Are we better off?

I do not know. My most acute memory—getting used to people coming into the stores with masks on in a line of such violence. My heart would jump and I expected a gun from every one of them. I'm sure better off on that."

All 4 joined in the laughter, just as his wife arrived with a picnic basket for lunch. Her name was Clara and she and Red met during Covid19. She was a nurse. When queried as she unpacked lunch. "Of course, I'm better off. I could not marry that Red-haired man at the end of the table until it was over for the medical staff because I was so involved with patients. He is much easier to live with and I have lovely in-laws and a new house. Whoopee."

Red took charge again. I know we want to hear our two other people here, but I personally am starving and as his plate reached him, he signed and said, "Prepare for a taste of heaven. She made enchilada casserole and the other fixings. Pass another round of Cervesa, Junior."

Silence reigned for 10 minutes. Then Junior said, "I think these enchiladas are a perfect background for Pedro to tell us his story, and I'm sure it will be quite a story."

Pedro smiled and said, if in many ways, it is the saddest story. We were the poor side of the family working in my uncle's ranches. All of us worked and worked hard—no breaks for being nephews. He had two big fruit orchards and arrangements with a market chain that ran their fresh produce departments. Our family worked in the orchards—I started at 10. My cousins albeit older, worked in the markets with other sons and daughters from his wife's family. Our family of five lived in a two-bedroom cottage in one of the orchards—then came Corona.

The first blow came early in the pandemic. We thought it was nothing. Every migrant worker my uncle had, took off for Central America, their home trying to escape the virus. They just spread it in Costa Rica and Guatemala. Before they left, however, one of them must have worked with my oldest cousin, the one who was supposed to take over the whole operation. He became very sick and died. Then one by one, each of my Uncle's children died from Covid-19.

My aunt had a breakdown. She had spent many hours at her church when it began and increasingly more time there as it progressed. Her one surviving daughter joined her there and they spent every day by the statue of Mary. Eventually Margareta, her daughter, joined a convent. The strain was getting to my uncle, and he sent for my dad who was his much younger brother. There must have been 20 years between them.

Dad was ambitious and had been taking business classes at the junior college. He was just what my uncle needed. We moved from the orchard into a real house in Calexico. One by one, we took over the retail produce operations. It was a wonderful change, but Covid-19 was growing, as you remember, I am sure. In the five years we were learning our trade, it went from an occasional death to daily reports on the news of death tolls in the 100s. Then my uncle died and he left the retail end of his operation to my dad. The orchards went to their younger brother. The virus had taken all of Mother's children except me by this time. I was terrified of it. I took all the precautions—masks, gloves, jacket, and trousers that could be washed down every evening.

I was first in line for the vaccine when it came to one of our town operations. And so today I am a very wealthy man by our standard. That pickup is one of my cars. That pink house on the corner of Laguna and Chavez Streets is mine and so is the ranch house in the orchards. My young uncle sold them to me last year. But, I am lonesome. I have never had time to fall in love or find someone to marry. I want a family desperately. I cannot let my family die out. I am 39 and I shall be lucky if I can find the right person, someone like you, Clara."

"I've no sisters available, but a couple of very attractive nieces."

"Won't they think me too old?"

"Do you have any handy man skills?

"I can fix carpentry, plumbing, garden, and I can paint a house or a portrait. What do you need?"

The table broke into laughter. Another Friday Golf Session was a total success.

Made in the USA
Las Vegas, NV
09 November 2021